ESCORT TO TENDERNESS Preview

"Max," she gasped, sliding her hands up his chest to grip his shoulders. Ira rested her forehead against his temple and released a long sigh as his fingers began a caress. She'd not felt another's touch upon her body like this and was arrested with the indecision of what to do, how to feel. Ira was usually so protective of her personal space, and Max had been able to breach it with little effort. He'd disarmed her so smoothly, leaving her feeling exposed in a way she hadn't realized she'd clamored to experience. There was a freedom in such abject vulnerability; and maybe because he made a living in doing this, that he had experience and knew not to take such a thing for granted, that Ira allowed herself full rein to experience it too.

He'd guaranteed they'd go no further than she allowed. He wouldn't pressure her . . . wouldn't *judge* her.

Praise for Savannah J. Frierson

"The emotional connection between the hero and heroine was superb."

Book Riot on *Trolling Nights*

"Reading *Be Mine* was like sinking into spicy candyfloss . . . There is nothing I love more than books that are both erotic and achingly romantic, and this one ticked that box."

Talia Hibbert, author of *Act Your Age, Eve Brown*, on *Be Mine*

"I loved this beautifully written, sexy and moving novelette . . ."

Ruby Lang, author of *Open House*, on "Grounded for Christmas"

"It deserves all the stars and then some."

Romance Novels in Color on *Being Plumville*

Escort to Tenderness

A TROLLING NIGHTS Novel

Savannah J. Frierson

To having all the tenderness we deserve and desire.

ESCORT TO TENDERNESS

One

The corner of the business card Ira Jackson held created a divot in her index finger, breaking up the clay that had hardened there from that afternoon's throwing session. Biting her lower lip, she looked at the handwritten blocky numbers on the back of the card, numbers that would lead to the person whose name was embossed on the front. Max Worthington, one of her cousin Gideon's dearest friends and the person she hoped could help with her current predicament.

"Oh, predicament, Ira?" she chastised herself. "This is not some earth-shattering, life-ending matter. It's an irritation *at most*."

Ira ignored her internal side-eye at the claim. For people with sense and perspective, her *irritation* was exactly that, a fact about her life that chafed when something brushed against it, and this "something" had been brushing up for a while—long before she'd ever met a Max Worthington.

Toward the end of their brief introduction a few months back, he'd told her to call her when she was ready, and "ready" for her meant when she'd gathered enough courage to have him help her fulfill a dream experience. But after months of going back and forth, of filling her inner stores with courage before letting them spill out and empty again, she'd promised herself the next time those stores filled, she'd throw on the lids, lock them up, and call Max *right then and there*.

But she really wanted to call her sister and her cousin first.

Too bad Murphy was currently in Europe on tour with her jazz quartet while Gideon was getting pretty for the cameras on a photo shoot in the Bahamas—both last-minute, once-in-a-lifetime opportunities a thirty-first birthday should never supersede—but now she was on the precipice of throwing herself at a near stranger?

Ira rolled her eyes at herself. "Happy birthday, indeed."

She wasn't a toddler despite her inner child throwing a tantrum at the moment. Besides, what would she know about an artistic, jet-setting life? She was rarely jealous of her sister and cousin, but their lives were so dynamic and fun, always on the move. Hers was so static and slow the tortoise had already lapped her twice and the hare was gearing up for the next race. Her world was full of schedule and stability, but at least being an intake nurse provided some adrenaline rushes. One truly never knew what kind of injury or sickness would come through those urgent care doors next.

Ira squared her shoulders. "You're doing this, girl, once and for all."

Blowing out a breath, she lifted her eyes from the business card to her computer monitor, rubbing her left hand over the closely cropped curls atop her head. The feel of her natural tight coils soothed her as the site for Dream Dude LLC filled her vision.

An escort service website.

Max's escort service website.

She blinked at the provocative poses of mostly shirtless men with their come-hither stares and too-perfect everythings. They were *not* the dudes she dreamed of whenever she went to sleep. Nevertheless, with shoulders still squared, Ira began perusing the Dream Dudes with a determined expression on her face. Yet that determination began withering and crumbling the more she looked. Some—*most*—were too pretty . . . too *perfect.* Intellectually, she understood why clients would go for them, but the conventional flawlessness they presented left her feeling *meh.*

Ira snorted at her gall. "Look at you picky!"

She hadn't been on a date in nigh six years, having grown disillusioned with her numerically limited options in the South Carolina Lowcountry. Gideon had always accused her of having too-high standards, but Ira could only like what she liked. She was personable, friendly enough, and understood her generous ass could compensate for the "generosity" everywhere else on her. But since the people she'd dated hadn't sparked anything beyond an amiable feeling if she were lucky, she'd decided to focus more on her career instead.

Or rather, the one she wanted it to be.

Though she currently worked as an intake nurse at the town's one urgent care center to pay the bills, Ira squirreled enough away to pay for studio time to throw clay. She made ceramics, really nice ones if the small stable of clients she'd gained had anything to say about it. Besides, throwing clay was such a soothing, productive way to wind down from the workday.

Her cousin and sister thought she could quit her job and pursue her art full time, the way they were pursuing theirs, but turning down a decent, steady paycheck for a passion seemed peak irresponsible. She wasn't the beauty Gideon was or the talented musician Murphy was. Ira had only been doing ceramics for two years; that wasn't nearly a long enough track record to make that switch feasible. Then again, most of her disposable income, the little she had, *did* go to studio time and supplies. If she made this an official business, at least those expenses could become deductions at tax time.

Ira huffed and shook her head before snickering. "I am on a website full of attractive men, and I'm *still* thinking about my money moves?" Her snicker turned into a derisive laugh. "If this ain't proof I needed to call Max ASAP, I don't know what is!"

Refocusing, Ira began scanning the men's names instead of their bodies. She did click on some, especially ones underneath the few men of color featured. Then Ira blanched at their rates. The least expensive was two hundred dollars an hour, with pre-decimal-point zeros being added the longer the time was requested.

"The hell!"

Now she *really* felt some kind of way. She wished she could call Gideon or Murphy for a come-to-Jesus meeting. Things had been picking up with her ceramics projects, but could she truly splurge on a Dream Dude at *these* rates? One night alone would cost more than her monthly rent, and she wasn't prepared to drop that much money on a date that might not even go well.

She shook her head, covering her face with her hands. "Nope! That is not the energy with which we're approaching this, Ira."

She shouldn't think that way. Hell, maybe thinking that way had doomed her previous dates at the start. It would be nice to do something adventurous on her birthday for once, instead of the customary movie and milkshake she'd been treating herself to these past few years. Even last year for her big 3-0 she'd been fairly pedestrian, although treating herself to an all-day throwing session at the studio and a nice take-home dinner from a local Italian restaurant had been a highlight. She'd even taken off work to celebrate, giving herself a nice, three-day weekend since it'd fallen on a Friday. Her sister and cousin had been slated to come celebrate with her, but Gideon had gotten sick days before, just as Murphy had booked a career-breaking gig with a major jazz star Ira had insisted she not relinquish for the sake of her thirtieth birthday.

She scoffed at her dramatics. "A regular martyr, you are."

Ira pressed her hand between her ample thighs, liking the softness and warmth they provided, and bit her lip again. Was it wrong to want another hand there for once, and for more than comfort? A strong, masculine one that knew how to touch a body. What would be the harm in this? She was grown, officially on the other side of thirty come the weekend. Why not learn a bit about what Dream Dude LLC actually was?

HoIra checked the time on her smartphone. It was a little after eight. Not too late, but it was a Tuesday night, and maybe Max had things to do? If he did, she'd just leave a message.

She wasn't chickening out again.

Licking her full lips, Ira unlocked the screen of her phone and pulled up the keypad. She typed in the area code, took a deep breath, then added the other seven digits.

"Max Worthington."

She gasped. She really and truly didn't mean to, but the bass in his voice was so resonant her entire body vibrated with it. How had she'd forgotten what his voice had done to her when they'd first met? Well, she hadn't, not really. She'd just shoved *that* into yet another box, right along with the memory of his lush-lipped smile, the slight blush in the apples of his pale cheeks as Gideon teased him during their introductions, and the Caesar-cut hairstyle of his dark-brown hair that managed to look adorable instead of outdated on him. She also remembered the way his rectangular, wire-framed glasses couldn't hide his kind green eyes and the way his tailored suit molded his tall, buff frame that belied his past as an athlete—

"Ira?"

She cleared her throat, hoping she managed not to sound raspy or aroused as she finished quaking at her name riding on the soundwaves of his voice. "Yes, hi—wait, how did you know it was me?"

He chuckled. She bit her tongue to stifle a whimper, squeezing her thighs around the hand that was still there. She didn't know what the hell was going on, but if it could stop post-haste, that would be *great*. She had such a thing for voices—the deeper, the better—but something about Max's voice hooked her and refused to let go.

"Gideon," Max said on the ending hills of his laugh. "She gave me your number. Put it in my phone, actually. She's an . . . *assertive* person at times, so, you know, no stopping her."

Ira huffed. "You're too kind. Everyone else just says bossy."

"You said it, not me," Max confirmed, another laugh floating on the line. "But I'm glad she did. I don't answer calls from people I don't know, especially after business hours."

"You *did* give me your personal number. On a business card," Ira reminded him.

"Excellent point. And to think if not for Gideon, I would've missed you. I'll thank her profusely next time I see her."

As she looped "*would've missed you*" in her mind like the thirsty heffa she was, Ira picked up the hint of a Southern accent she hadn't noticed before. It didn't sound like what she was used to hearing in her town, but the way he stretched out some words and ended others—consonants optional—implied his home region.

"Yes, well." Ira cringed, having no idea how to segue from pleasantries to the purpose of her call. She guessed there was nothing to do but jump. "This is about business, so should I call tomorrow morning?"

"I have a feeling if I let you go, you won't call me again." His voice was warmer, almost like the teasing Gideon had given him during their introductions. "So, let's talk shop now. I've been hoping you'd call, actually."

"*Really*?" She winced at the audible shock in her tone. "I mean, um, 'really?'"

This time the chuckle was more of a laugh, and she accepted the fact it was at her expense. "Yes."

"That eager for a new client?"

"No. Well, not *just* that. A new friend, too, yes?"

Well, that was what she got for trying to tease him back, huh? "Oh."

"Yes," he said again, and humor crept back into his voice. "Besides, I just won a bet. Gideon didn't think you'd even call, but I knew you would."

Ira didn't know whether to feel embarrassed at him clocking her like that or smug that she'd proven her baby cousin wrong. "Why were you so sure?"

"Because I'm arrogant enough to think I'm a good conversationalist?"

Ira laughed loud at that. "Seriously!"

"No," Max said, laughing himself, "although I do think I'm good at that too. But more, I really wanted to do this for you. But you had to make that decision, and the last thing I will ever do is hard sell a friend."

"I'm a friend?"

"Acquaintance is too stale. Maybe friend by proxy, then? Gideon loves you and I love Gideon, so I'd assumed we'd get along once we really started talking. How's it been going for you so far?"

She smiled. "So far, so good, surprisingly. I was nervous."

"That's understandable."

"I've never used an escort service before."

"I'm happy to answer whatever questions you have. Part of the reason I gave you my direct number."

Ira nodded and blew out a breath. "Okay, then. I guess the first question is: how does this all work? With your, um, 'Dudes' and your clients?"

"My Dream Dudes will be whoever they need to be to make a client's time pleasant."

"So, they're actors?"

He laughed again. "Some of them. But all of them are attentive. They won't be rude; and if the Date isn't going well, then it'll end early, and Dream Dudes will prorate the fee. Can't get paid the full amount if they don't stay, you know."

"That's fair."

"We aim to be," Max said. "Dream Dude LLC is all about making sure our clients get exactly the experience they want, but we know what's on paper doesn't always translate in person. I don't believe in penalizing people just because a connection isn't made."

"What if the person is being rude or obnoxious?"

"The Dude or the client?"

"Either?"

"If it's the Dude, he's fired, and the client gets a full refund. If it's the client, then they're put on a probationary ban, and they don't get that Date's fee refunded. First and foremost is respect, Ira. It must be mutually given."

With those words, a great bulk of her anxiety eased out of her system. She exhaled slowly and nodded, even though Max couldn't see her. "Do you get clients of all shapes, sizes, walks of life?"

"Yes," Max said. "I know the rates can be high for some Dudes, and that's because they tend to be the most popular, but we have a referral service. Sometimes we even do promotional Dates."

She was feeling more relaxed the more she heard. Maybe she *could* have this experience for herself, except she didn't see any current promotions on the site.

"Okay. Well, all of this has been elucidating. Thank you."

He chuckled. "There's a vast misconception about the services an escort provides. I'll spare you that spiel right now in favor of asking you, who is your Dream Dude?"

"I don't have one," she blurted. She internally groaned and dropped her forehead into her palm. Why had she said it like that?

"Really? No ideal date with an ideal partner?"

"No." Shame slithered through her. Maybe it was more accurate to say she didn't think she'd ever find an ideal partner, so she didn't bother thinking about one.

"Hmm. You're presenting me with a challenge. I like that." He went silent for a moment. "I think we need to figure that out before we go forward—actually, do you mind getting on camera?"

Her earlier anxiety hadn't gone far because it leaped back inside. "Why?"

"It'll help me get a read on you, and then you can get a read on me too. This isn't a one-way interaction, after all."

"Do you do this with all of your nervous, potential clients?"

"I do offer it as an option," he said, "although it's not me who's usually doing these interviews."

"Don't I feel special?"

"That *is* the goal of a Dream Date."

She laughed, starting to relax again. His voice could be as soothing as it was arousing. Really, what would be the harm?

"That seems to be the question of the night," she muttered to herself.

"I'm sorry?"

"I said, that should be all right," Ira amended aloud. She looked down at the top she wore, a white tank splotched with gray and brown clay. She should change her shirt. She then eyed the foot of the bed where there were clothes draped on the comforter. Laundry she'd yet to put away. She would *not* dress up, but she would put on a clean shirt.

Except, the screen flashed, and the video chat request popped up on her computer monitor. Ira considered it for a moment, then shrugged and accepted it. Max might as well get the authentic Ira right from the top.

Two

When Ira's face appeared on the screen, Max Worthington couldn't help the smile that appeared. He remembered his first impression of her when he'd met her at Gideon's birthday party months ago, and it remained the same with this second one. He felt instantly warm in her presence, a comfort he hadn't known for far too long.

She had a mature voice with a tone and drawl that reminded him of molasses, and the face that went with it was just as sweet. It was smooth, dark, and round, with big dark-brown eyes that regarded him with wary interest. Her lips were full and dark, too, and much, much too kissable.

He clenched his hand around the mouse to keep from reaching for the screen when she smiled shyly at him, a hint of apology in her eyes.

"You're in a suit, and I look like I've just been through the wringer."

"You look lovely." He let his eyes drift from her face to the rest of what was visible. She appeared smooth all over, with prominent collarbones that helped support her long neck and sturdy shoulders. The deep-brown hue of her skin made the white tank top she wore pop in the most alluring way.

"Is that clay?" He drew a line along his chest, and she looked down at hers to light brown streak on the slope of her chest near one of the tank's straps.

She groaned. He smiled wider.

"I knew I should've changed."

"No, it's fine." He nodded. "I remember you telling me you did ceramics. Gideon showed me some pictures too. Your art is amazing."

Her scowl transformed into a smile, making her cheeks turn into apples. "Thank you."

He smoothed a hand over his mouth and nodded again, licking his lips behind his palm. The same question plagued him now as it had when he'd first met her: Did she taste as sweet as she looked?

"So, your Dream Dude. What's he like?"

She gave a helpless shrug along with a self-conscious laugh. "Someone nice?"

"That's standard," he replied, shaking his head. "What else? What would make this person exactly right for *you*? Who do you dream about?"

"Nobody."

"Really?"

She shrugged again. "I've put it so far out of my mind and focus that I'm hoping it'll be one of those things that I'll know when I see it."

Max pursed his lips. This was a complication with some potential clients. Often, they weren't in the dating pool, so they were essentially starting from scratch. But he was also judging the hell out of Charleston. How had no one seen the jewel she was? If he hadn't been convinced earlier, with Gideon waxing such poetic about her and then their brief introduction in person, this interaction would've done it. Ira didn't have an artificial bone in her body, and she really did seem incredibly sweet—a wonderful balance to her cousin's spice.

"You don't play games," he said after another moment, and smiled when she scoffed and rolled her eyes.

"Who has the time?" she asked, and he heard the genuineness in her tone. "Not to mention it's annoying. Say what you say and mean what you mean. If I wanted to read between the lines, I'd pick up an annotated novel!"

He sputtered out a laugh, which made her duck her head and laugh too.

"What kind of novel?" he asked once they settled.

She shrugged. "I don't know. Maybe James Baldwin, or Richard Wright—no, Zora."

"Zora?"

"Neale Hurston," Ira clarified. "She wrote *Their Eyes Were Watching God* and *Jonah's Gourd Vine*. I'd check them out if you're not familiar with her work."

He nodded. "I will. The other authors you named too."

She smiled. "Are you a reader?"

He shrugged, then shook his head. "Not really, at least not novels. I like biographies, though."

Ira nodded. "A lot of people aren't, and I think the busier you are, the less likely you will be. It's all good, though. But, if you want to ease back into some novels, I wouldn't start with those three."

"Oh, who would you start with?"

She screwed up her lips in a contemplative expression. "Maybe Walter Mosley? You look like a guy who could appreciate a good mystery."

He nodded. That didn't sound too heavy. "Thanks for the suggestion."

"You're welcome!"

"I think the same for you, actually," he said, bringing them back on topic. "You need to be eased back into dating."

"Uh . . . okay?"

He grinned. He'd made this decision before he'd even left Gideon's birthday party, but this conversation had confirmed it'd been the right one. "How about me? Let *me* be your Dream Dude."

Her eyebrows rose and her mouth dropped open, but he dared not laugh at her shocked expression. It was a long moment before she gathered herself. "Is this something you suggest to all of your potential clients?"

He shook his head. He couldn't tell her he'd been charmed from the first, could he? That he'd realized he hadn't wanted anyone else from Dream Dudes to give her the Dream Date she would deserve. That would come across as creepy.

"No, but I feel doubly responsible for you."

"Yikes."

Max barely stopped himself from knocking his head on his desk. "Yeah, that sounded way worse out loud than it did in my head." He had to turn this around, and fast! "What I mean is, you're the family of a dear friend, and I want this to be a great experience for you. I'm not exactly a matchmaker by training, but I've been doing this long enough that I can help you figure out what you'd like in a Dream Dude for a Dream Date."

Her eyes narrowed, and she regarded him for a long moment. "And what would that entail exactly?"

He looked down at his keyboard with a frown, realizing he didn't really know. "Have you ever been to Miami?"

"Nope."

He nodded. "Want to go?"

Ira's eyes widened again. "What? When!"

He shrugged. "Whenever. You can stay at my place or get a hotel."

"With you?"

He shrugged again. "Most overnight dates have the client and the Dude together, but we don't have to be. Whatever's comfortable for you."

"But your place?"

"My condo has two bedrooms, and both have their own bathrooms. They're on opposite ends of the hall, too, so you'd have relative privacy."

She blinked. "And you're okay with sharing a space with a stranger?"

"I don't really consider you a stranger," he said honestly. "Friend by proxy, remember?"

She looked off to the side, her hand going to her chest as if her heart hurt. He ran back over what he said, hoping he hadn't inadvertently caused her pain. Was the offer too generous? Too forward? She hadn't even explicitly stated she wanted any of this, let alone with him. Was he pushing too hard?"

"My birthday's this weekend."

Her quiet confession was like a key clicking loudly into its lock. Now he wanted her to come to Miami just so she wouldn't spend it alone. She hadn't had to say that she would be otherwise; her tone screamed that fact.

"I'll get you a ticket," Max said, his tone brooking no argument. "It's your birthday. I'd like for it to be as special as it can be even if your loved ones aren't here to share in the day."

She dropped her head then, and he watched her shoulders rise and fall in measured intervals, her hand tightening into a fist at her chest.

"That's so kind," she said, her voice a little hoarse.

Max's own throat became surprisingly thick. He cleared it. "No problem. I've spent enough birthdays alone to know sometimes, you just want a friend on your day."

"We've upgraded from friend-by-proxy to friend, period, huh?" she asked, a half-smile forming on her sweet face.

His smile was automatic in response to hers. "I'd like us to." *For a start*, he finished to himself, then looked down sharply at that rogue thought.

"Everything okay?"

"Yeah," he said absently, glaring at the trembling hands he'd shoved into his lap. He'd been in the presence of a beautiful woman before; hell, he was often surrounded by them. New York, Miami, LA—he was charming and now wealthy, a far cry from the white, abandoned trailer trash he'd been in his youth. He'd been able to keep the necessary distance with the people he was attracted to in his line of work, to the point it'd been years since he'd been in an actual relationship and over one year since he'd been intimate with someone. Neither had been a conscious choice, but work and lack of real interest were powerful inhibitors.

Ira Jackson being able to break through them so quickly and effortlessly shook him.

She leaned closer to her monitor, making her dark, round face appear larger in the screen. He now noticed flecks of copper in her dark-brown eyes. He found himself leaning forward, too, as if waiting for her to spill a secret. She suddenly grimaced and snickered.

"I don't know why I'm leaning forward like this an actual window. Ridiculous!"

The tension inside of him sprung out in a guffaw, and Max threw back his head with the force of it. He could hear her giggle, which made him laugh harder. Tears seeped out the corners of his eyes and he curled halfway into a ball in his executive office chair. The black leather squeaked as he rocked, chortling like a loon, and he wiped his tears with the forearm of his gray-blue dress shirt.

"Oh, my God," he said as he began to simmer down. "That was the funniest thing I've seen in weeks!"

"I'm glad I could brighten your day," Ira deadpanned, but a smile remained on her face.

"Now you have to let me return the favor for you this weekend."

She screwed up her lips again, and it was just as adorable now as it'd been before. He wanted this so badly, for her, yes, but also for himself. She was someone who deserved to be cherished, adored, and pampered. But a small part of him couldn't help but think all of the knowledge and experience he'd gained by being in this business had been mean for this moment—

This *woman.*

She hid her face behind her hands and did a little shimmy. "I can't believe I'm about to say yes?"

He gripped the edge of the desk, needing to keep himself grounded . . . sane. He felt they were on the brink of something major, but Ira would have to take the leap for both of them.

"Is that a question or your final answer?"

Three

It was a sunny and comfortable eighty-degree early evening when Ira stepped off the train with her roller suitcase in one hand and her smartphone in the other. She'd been texting Murphy and Gideon all train ride—or rather, they'd been texting *her*, and she'd been responding to their inquisition. Gideon was beside herself with joy over the fact she'd taken such a leap whereas Murphy, in between her musical sets and traveling from Germany to Belgium, lectured her on her impulsiveness and how she'd fly to the Bahamas and maim Gideon herself should something happen to her older sister.

"Murph, the only thing that *should* happen is a moratorium on Ira's celibacy!"

Ira hadn't even responded to that, turning the phone's screen dark and taking a much-needed nap.

However, she'd promised to text them when she'd arrived in the city, and she was keeping that vow now. The missive was short and to the point, and then hummingbirds took wing in her stomach when her phone vibrated with an incoming text that wasn't from Gideon or Murphy.

I see you.

Trembling accompanied the flutters, and she looked around until she locked eyes with a pair of moss green ones that had become so incredibly familiar in such a short amount of time. Max grinned as he began his approach, and she pocketed her phone while she walked toward him too.

Though Ira had remembered he was tall, he was much more giant than man. He managed to make her five-eight frame feel tiny compared to him. He still rocked that '90s-era Caesar haircut that somehow managed to look adorable on him, softening his appearance and giving him an almost cherubic look thanks to his peaches-and-cream complexion. His rectangular glasses, bracketing a narrow nose that hovered above full, pink lips, really were the perfect shape for his square face and still couldn't obscure those stunning eyes of his. And to round off all that loveliness, he was smiling at her.

Even the slight crookedness of his bottom front teeth was endearing.

"Hey there," he greeted once they reached each other.

"Hi." She was unsure about what the protocol would be here. They'd spoken via webcam nearly all week, both of them unwilling or unable to say goodnight until she'd finally fall asleep at her keyboard. After the first night, she'd awakened to a dark screen and a text from him saying he'd see her tomorrow evening, and that she had the cutest snore he'd ever heard. Embarrassment had shared a place with giddiness inside of her; but she'd returned every night to talk to him, asking him questions about what she should expect. She'd even stayed up last night, both to get herself so tired that she'd sleep on the train and because, well, she *liked* talking to Max.

Ultimately, Ira held out a hand for him to shake, but he didn't. Instead, he grasped her hand and held it for a moment. His was large, warm, and oddly comforting around hers. Ira inhaled deeply, feeling languid. Maybe the lack of sleep and the long travel was catching up to her because she had the strangest urge to cuddle into his big body and take a nap. His presence was that soothing.

He smiled so his eyes crinkled and squeezed her hand before letting go. "You look fit to sleep where you stand." He took the luggage from her. "It's a decent thirty-minute drive from here to my condo, but I'll hope for some traffic for you so you can sleep a bit longer."

"That's really considerate of you," Ira said, following after him. He kept his stride at an easy pace, seamlessly navigating the crowds with an occasional polite "Excuse me" and grins. Heads turned to look at him and his commanding presence. Good to know she wasn't the only one dazed by him.

He stopped at a gleaming cherry-red Mustang GT convertible. Ira had to clamp her mouth with her hand to muffle her gasp, but his amused grin told her she hadn't been quite successful at being unheard.

"Are you a car girl?" he asked, opening the passenger-side door and helping her get settled. The butter-soft black leather seats cradled her like she was an infant.

"Not as such," she admitted. "But this is a sweet-looking ride."

He shut her door, and Ira looked in her side-view mirror to see him placing her suitcase in the car's trunk. The sun felt nice coming through the window, and she rested her head against the glass to bask in it, closing her eyes.

She stirred a little when Max entered the car, and he looked at her with yet another smile.

"All right?" he asked, buckling his seatbelt.

She did the same, his action reminding her she hadn't done so yet, and nodded. "Yes. Again, thank you for your generous hospitality."

"My pleasure," he said, bringing the car to life. The vehicle was smooth, yet powerful as Max maneuvered it onto the street. She felt as if they were gliding down the road.

"I still can't believe I did this," Ira continued. "I'm never this bold. That's Gideon's territory!"

"Well, let me be the first to say bold looks good on you, Miss Ira."

She yawned around a smile. They were now on a stretch of freeway, and the lull of a constant speed made her eyes droop. "Ugh, I should've slept more on the train!"

Max laughed lightly. "You don't have to stay awake to keep me company. Close those beautiful brown eyes of yours and gets some rest. We have all weekend to get to know each other."

She shivered in anticipation of this but gave herself over to the travel fatigue. Unfortunately, she'd just started to get a good sleep in when she felt the car stop and heard the gentle call of her name.

She slowly cracked one eye open. "Five more minutes."

He grinned but shook his head. "There's a much more comfortable bed waiting for you inside, Ira. Let's try that out."

She hummed even as she snuggled further into the car seat, closing her eyes again. "It must be a cloud if it beats this!"

He laughed. "It does. I promise. Give it a shot?"

She peeled her eyes back open and looked at him, then at their surroundings. They were in front of glass double doors underneath a high porte-cochere. A valet was standing by her door, ready to open it so she could disembark, and she straightened.

"Whoops, I'm keeping the man from doing his job!"

"Nothing like that," Max assured her, and he opened his car door. This apparently signaled the valet, for he opened her door too. Ira thanked the valet and began to rifle through her purse for a few dollars.

"What are you doing?" Max asked her.

"Ah," Ira said absently, still looking for the bills she *knew* she had, but then a strong, pale hand covered hers. She inhaled a shuddering breath. The warmth was still there, filling her spirit with a feeling that had eluded her until his touch. Going for broke, Ira flipped her hand underneath his, catching the now-freed wallet with her other hand, until they were palm to palm. To her relief and delight, he squeezed her hand gently.

"I don't want to see that wallet for the rest of the trip," he said with a teasing lilt, but Ira suspected he was completely serious.

"I thought clients paid everything on Dream Dates."

"Not this time," he determined, giving her a half grin. "It's your birthday weekend. This is my gift to you."

"Isn't that a bit zero-to-sixty considering the newness of our friendship?"

Max shrugged. "I won't mind if you don't."

She focused on the hold of her hand in his, how secure she felt, like he wouldn't and couldn't steer her wrong. Her cousin and sister had always said she had good instincts about people, and her buzzer of alarm had yet to go off while with Max. Besides, Gideon *was* his friend.

For all of her gregariousness, Gideon wasn't a slouch in the instincts department herself.

"I won't mind, then, either," she promised, placing the wallet back in her purse.

"Good," he replied, and with a final squeeze, let go of her hand. He pulled out his own wallet and gave a few bills to the valet. He then took Ira's suitcase with a personable nod.

The hummingbirds returned as the car drove off.

Max smiled at her. "Ready?"

Ira nodded, approaching him so they could enter the condo high-rise's lobby together. The space was sleek, modern, with wood browns and golds dominating the color scheme. She felt as if she were in a contemporary art museum, so different from the nineteenth-century antebellum look that Lowcountry South Carolina favored so much. He led them to a set of elevators that seemed different from the primary bank, and she arched an eyebrow at him.

"Penthouse?"

Max snorted. "Hardly. I'm a respectable 38th floor, thank you."

"Out of?"

"Fifty, I think."

She smirked but said nothing, preceding him into the elevator. They stood close but not touching as the car zoomed upwards, the ride smooth and incredibly quick.

She blinked in surprise when the doors opened to a small foyer where a sleek, black console table sat directly across from them, with a large smooth bronze vase set on top with decorative branches snaking out of it. There was also a black phone on one end and an umbrella rack on the other side of the table on the floor, which looked to be the same gleaming wood as the main lobby downstairs. The elevator doors began to ding, snapping her from her daze, and she quickly disembarked.

She ignored Max's light laugh behind her.

"Door's on the right," he murmured. There was a keypad on his door, and he passed her to put in a code. She looked around the space, surprised by the floor-to-ceiling window showcasing a sunset-graced Miami at the foyer's opposite end.

"The view's better inside."

"I'll bet," she muttered under her breath, but managed to tear her eyes away from that view to enter his condo.

Damn the man, but he was right. Two of the three walls of his main living space were windows that offered large, sweeping views of a bay and more of Miami. She could see a stadium in the near distance and bridges linking the city to landmasses in the bay and beyond. The setting sun behind them cast everything in an orange and purple glow. She'd been sleepy, but this spectacular view offered a second wind.

"Do you want to go on the balcony?"

Max held open the door to the balcony for her and she stepped out onto it. There was a light breeze that brushed along her skin, creating goosebumps. Car horns, the sounds of accelerating engines, and even some peals of laughter made it up to their level, and Ira let the city's vibrancy invigorate her senses.

"This view is absolutely breathtaking," she said.

"I couldn't agree more."

She took in the view for one final moment before looking back at Max. His eyes were riveted on her, rooting her to the spot. Yet her heart felt free and loopy like a balloon in the wind.

Four

Takeout from Max's favorite Cuban restaurant would be their dinner tonight. Max scooped portions of rabo encendido and white rice into two bowls and stuck a spoon in each. There was also an uncorked bottle of Chardonnay in the fridge that he wouldn't open until he knew Ira wanted wine or would be okay if he had some without her.

He placed the dishes onto the set dining table, he at the head and she perpendicular to him. Although, she might be more comfortable on the patio, as she was still knocked out.

The second wind she'd gained from her initial visit to the balcony had waned almost as quickly as it'd arrived. She'd claimed she'd wanted to sit on the chaise to have a more comfortable spot from which to take in the view, but she'd been out in the space of two breaths. She hadn't even stirred when he'd draped a blanket over her, her face just as relaxed as it'd looked when she'd fall asleep mid-conversation during their late-night talks this week.

He smiled, remembering how she'd deny her tiredness and valiantly try to maintain a meandering conversation with him. Maybe, *perhaps*, she'd felt the same tug he'd felt as when they spoke. It'd only grown stronger, tauter, as their discussions transitioned from one topic to the next. She had fantastic and gross stories about her job as an intake nurse; and, of course, he had fascinating tales of his own occupation as an escort-turned-CEO of one of the most in-demand escort services in the country. She'd tried to ask him questions about how he'd even started the company, but he'd deftly redirected the topic back to her. She still hadn't *really* answered the question of whom her Dream Dude was and what kind of Dream Date she'd like to have, even though he'd asked her each night they'd talked. Yet they were finally sharing space, so Max thought now would be a good opportunity to glean some answers.

He already had one—Ira liked someone who could keep her warm when the world became too cold.

"Who didn't?" Max muttered to himself, ignoring the way his heart throbbed at the maudlin thought.

Dusk had settled upon the city, the sky more purple than gold now. Edges of Ira's blanket swayed gently in the breeze and still, she slept. He hated to awaken her, but he was certain she was hungry. Unbeknownst to her, he'd heard her stomach rumble softly on the drive to his condo while she'd dozed. He would be a poor host if he didn't provide sustenance.

He eyed the unlit white tapers in the center of the table and decided to keep them unlit. He thought that might cast too intimate a tableau. Hell, maybe even the table did. He'd eat on the balcony if she preferred it, but he'd at least wanted to show her he could and would be mannerly.

Flipping on the outside light, Max stepped onto the balcony. Ira hadn't moved, still asleep, so he crouched down to his haunches and placed a careful hand on her shoulder. Ira didn't startle awake, but she did shift away from his touch and burrow deeper into the chair. Smiling softly, he shook her shoulder again. Her eyes fluttered open this time.

"And Sleeping Beauty finally awakes," he teased, laughing when she rolled her eyes.

"Boy, bye with 'finally'!" she chastised with her own grin. "I'm only—what—half an hour into my hundred years of slumber. Cheatin' a gal out of some good sleep!"

He laughed more at that. "Did you ever stop to think your prince wouldn't take a hundred years to find you?"

"And you think it's you?" Ira asked, still teasing. "Can't be, seeing as you didn't even kiss me!"

"Maybe I'm so right for you I don't need to kiss you," Max bantered with a raised eyebrow.

Ira's smile became brittle, and her eyes dulled, her laugh reminding him of glass cracking. "So, cheated out of sleep *and* a kiss." She shook her head and snapped her fingers. "Happy birthday to me!"

She untangled herself from the blanket. Max stepped back to give her space to stand; but the moment she was on her feet, he was right in front of her. He could see the sheen in her eyes thanks to the balcony light, and he tipped his head down toward her.

"Are those things you'd like on your Date, Ira?" he asked quietly. "Sleep and a kiss?"

Her scoff was rough and angry, though at whom, Max couldn't be sure. "Who sleeps on a date?"

He shrugged. "I've had clients who've only wished to be held tenderly while they sleep. Comfort is a heady thing."

Ira looked down, placing hands on abundant hips. He watched her shoulders rise and fall with her deep intake of breath, and then her stomach grumbled again. She snickered this time, and he allowed the corners of his mouth to rise.

"An explanation for my crankiness," she said, then looked up with contrition in her eyes. "I'm sorry I snapped at you. Gideon and Murphy could tell you how much of a witch I become when my sugar gets low."

"I have dinner," Max said. "That's why I woke you up. I hope you like spice and oxtail."

She blinked. "I tend to steer clear of spice and I've never actually had oxtail."

He cringed, rubbing the back of his neck with a large palm. "Uh—"

"But I can try something new, Max," she assured him. "You must like it if you ordered it; and if you like it, it can't be all that bad, right?"

By the time dinner was over, it was safe to say Ira loved rabo encendido, even though she ended up with a mountain of crumpled napkins by her plate after blotting her reaction to the spice. Max discovered she was heat sensitive, not anti-heat, and Ira took her leaky nose in humorous, graceful stride. Max even found it endearing she had a glassful of milk instead of the more sophisticated Chardonnay while they ate, learning that milk helped cut down on the effects of spicy foods.

"Gideon's mom taught us that trick," Ira said with a grin, sitting across from Max at the kitchen island. He was rinsing off dishes and loading the dishwasher, *not* allowing Ira to help despite her insistence. She was a guest, and it was her birthday, after all. He'd had to promise he'd let her help the next time she visited to get her acquiescence, and then his heart had raced at the prospect of her being in his space like this again. Was it bad his heart raced in anticipation at the possibility?

"Gideon doesn't talk about her much," Max noted, looking over his shoulder at her. Ira averted her gaze for a moment. "Oh, I'm sorry—"

"Aunt Dot has a complicated relationship with most of us," Ira said with a false nonchalance he could hear. "Raised four children and only one chose a career she could understand. She's a magistrate judge in Moncks Corner, where we're from, but one kid's in the army; one's becoming a world-renowned musician; one's trying to be a future EGOT winner and pursuing modeling in the process. And then there's safe, predictable, intake-nurse me."

Max arched an eyebrow as he placed the last dish in the appliance before turning back and approaching the stove island where Ira sat. He dried his hands with a dish towel. "Would you or anyone else predict you being here in Miami with me? A man you've only spoken a few times before for an entire weekend?"

Her smile was impish and a little proud. "No."

He smiled as well and nodded. "I'll say this, though: you are safe with me, Ira. Dream Dude is all about consent—nothing happens the client doesn't wish to happen, nor do we coerce you into doing something you don't want to do."

She regarded him with a contemplative look. "What does it say about the state of our society that you have to reassure me with something that should be a given?"

He shrugged. "People can be animals."

"Ain't that the truth."

"And I try not to be." Max felt himself sink into memories best forgotten and shuddered. His mind filled with images of a red-soaked linoleum floor; sounds of water rushing into the sink with dull, staccato thuds, the feel of the slick legs of the table he'd hidden beneath and gripped when the yelling and punching had commenced. The sight of dusty, heavy boots that left muddy, then bloody footprints on the kitchen floor as they thumped out the ramshackle mobile home, never to return.

"Max?"

He squeezed his eyes shut then relaxed his hands from around the dish towel he'd been strangling. He cleared his throat, but it remained gruff despite himself. "Sorry. Kinda drifted there."

Ira's eyes were full of empathy. "I apologize for sending you wherever you went." She frowned. "Not to get in your business, but if you need an ear . . ."

He nodded, not looking at her, and folded the dish towel carefully before draping it on the oven's handle. Hell, *he* might be the one who needed to be held for a spell, and Ira looked like she could give kickass hugs. She was plush and smelled like pineapples, maybe from whatever lotion or cream she used during her daily ablutions.

Dark-brown hands entered his field of vision and tapped a quick rhythm on the cold stovetop. He smiled and, before he could catch himself, grasped her hands. There was lingering clay on some of her fingers, and he rubbed the pad of his thumb over one splotch.

"Would you like pottery studio time?"

Max didn't look at Ira as he asked the question, his thumb now surveying the smoothness of her short nails. They were unpainted but neatly clipped, topping off fingers that were long and elegant. He could imagine these hands creating works of art.

"Uh . . ."

He looked up at her now, and her eyes were heavy-lidded as they regarded their hands. Going on a hunch, Max threaded their fingers together and she curled hers gently around his, closing her eyes as she did. He watched her inhale deeply and exhale slowly, as if she were committing the sensation to memory for the times she'd be without his touch.

"You want tenderness, don't you?" Max asked softly. "That's your Dream Date."

Her fingers curled tighter around his, and then she let out a derisive snort. "Something so simple can be so hard to come by."

She started to pull back, but he firmed his hold. "I can do simple. I can give you simple."

Ira tugged her hands again, and this time Max let her go. She clasped her hands together and then rested them on her chest. She opened her mouth to speak, then frowned and pulled her bottom lip between her teeth. Max came around the island to her side of it but kept his distance. This reticence was familiar, having seen it in other potential clients before. But he couldn't think of Ira as a client. This was too intimate. Max wasn't sure if it was because she was the family of a friend, but he didn't *want* to treat her as just another client, either. He still felt like they were on the precipice of something.

Something *amazing*.

Belying his internal world-shaking revelations, he kept his face even and open, signaling for Ira to share, to reveal what she'd want for her weekend.

"But I don't want you to give me tenderness just as a favor for my birthday," she said, her voice strong despite her obvious nerves. "Shouldn't I earn that on my own?"

Max remained where he was despite his leg muscles vibrating with the urge to go to her. "What makes you think you haven't already?"

Five

Despite herself, Ira smiled at Max's words even as a thrill shot through her system. She tilted her head to the side and looked at him carefully, wanting visual confirmation of what her instincts were telling her: he meant his implication; he felt the connection between them as more than a quid pro quo.

Rationally, Ira recognized relationships began at the moment of meeting, no matter how they manifested. She just hadn't expected a potential romance for *her* to begin such a way. It was terrifying, really, standing on the brink of a fling the way she was, but Ira had to accept the fact *this* was the Dream Date she wanted—the rush of a whirlwind romance for just once in her life. And to have that experience within the safe parameters of a weekend and with someone who knew what he was doing—so much so he'd built a successful company on it—Ira didn't think she could've hit a bigger jackpot. She couldn't worry about what would happen on Monday. Friday through Sunday would be her sole point of focus.

She approached him and didn't stop until they were a mere breath apart. His green eyes had darkened, and she could feel the tension vibrating from him. Sighing deeply, Ira placed her hands on his broad chest and smiled softly at the feel of his heart pounding underneath her right palm.

"Can we do that, then?" she asked. "Can we hold each other through the night?"

He visibly swallowed and licked his lips. "Yeah," he said, his voice hoarse and he leaned forward, though still stopping short of touching her. "We can do that."

Ira nodded, unable to maintain eye contact with him any longer, and looked at his thick neck where she could see the furious beat of his pulse. She frowned at it, then jumped when his large hands settled upon her waist.

"Sorry," he apologized, immediately removing his hands.

She waved away his words. "No!" She laughed self-derisively. "I should get used to that. It just caught me off guard."

"Are you ticklish?"

Ira eyed him. "That's not why I jumped."

He cocked an eyebrow. "Is that a yes?"

She twisted her mouth against the smile that wouldn't be denied. "Will you use that yes against me?"

He shook his head. "Never against you, Ira."

She nodded at him, then gripped his hands and placed them on her plump waist. "Okay. I like how this feels too."

"Same here," Max replied, bringing her closer. "I like this even better."

The softness of her pressed against the granite of him, and Ira allowed her hands to slide up his chest and over his shoulders to clasp behind his neck. It was the typical embrace of preteens during their very first slow dance, and just like a preteen, Ira could barely look at Max in the eye without wanting to cheese and giggle. So she decided to go full bore, wrapping her arms so tightly around him that her breasts mashed against his chest, and her chin rested on his strong left shoulder. He leaned his temple against hers and began to smooth his hand along her back, taking his time between the hills and valleys her body had in a way that felt reverent, not ridiculing.

Ira didn't want to let go; she didn't want to be let go.

After a moment, Max groaned and buried his nose into the curve of her neck. Ira shivered. He gripped her tighter, and she began to stroke his nape, her fingers tangling in the silky curls there. She hummed at his light nuzzle under her jaw.

"I knew you'd give kickass hugs," he murmured into her skin, making her laugh and squeeze him tighter.

"And I'm not even the best in the family. That's Murphy. A Murphy hug is a straight blessing," Ira said, and finally ended the hug. Max's gaze was breathtakingly tender.

"I think I'll always prefer yours," he said sincerely, then smirked. "Especially compared to Gideon's."

Ira laughed. "She hugs like it's a chore, but everyone's not into those kinds of displays of affection." She looked around the space and then pointed between the two of them. "Her giving you my number was her way of showing she cared, probably for the both of us. Maybe if I talked to you, I'd book one of your Dudes as a return client, right?"

His smile dimmed but he nodded. "Makes sense."

His tone had grown cold, flinty. Ira shuddered and looked down the hall toward the stairs that must've led to the bedrooms. Every room on this floor was living and common areas.

"I think I should go to bed."

He nodded, still looking at her. "Where do you want this cuddle session to commence? Your room? Mine?"

"Mine."

Max nodded again, then held out his hand to Ira. "Let's get to it."

Ira grabbed her purse from the couch before taking his hand in hers. He guided her up the wood floating staircase to a wide landing. To their left was a corridor that Ira assumed was his bedroom. He led her right to an amply sized guest bedroom with a small walk-in closet and en-suite bathroom. The room's color scheme was steel blue and brown, with a queen platform bed flanked by stout brown nightstands that held an iHome alarm clock on one, a remote for the wall-mounted flat-screen television next to a smaller one on the other, and blue, oval lacquer lamps on both. The wall of floor-to-ceiling windows exposed the twinkling Miami landscape below. Her suitcase was at the foot of the bed already, and the bed looked as soft as a cloud. On the comforter was a stack of towels and washcloths for her to use.

"Good?"

"Yes. It's beautiful. The whole condo is. Thank you for hosting me," she said with a smile.

"I'll let you get settled. I'll check back in about thirty minutes in case you need anything."

Ira stood there for a moment completely bewildered after Max left. She had absolutely nothing that could be considered "sexy" by way of sleepwear in her suitcase. But did one wear "sexy" things to cuddle? Truth be told, she'd never done so in her life, and she pushed out the refrain of "Pathetic" that started to rev up in her mind.

Deciding to keep on as she would've if she'd had no bed partner for the night, Ira brushed and flossed her teeth, washed and moisturized her face, and donned the large green T-shirt that had been her cousin Jerome's once upon a time with black yoga pants. After a small debate, she went braless. She fully intended on falling asleep, and she was more comfortable without it. They were both adults, after all. And if Max's hands wandered . . . and Ira decided not to stop them . . . then that was their business.

She felt her face flame and was glad for her dark skin and solitude to blush in peace. Not bothering to suppress her wicked grin, Ira went to her purse and grabbed her phone, anxious for advice. Then she remembered Murphy was hours ahead of her and Gideon would probably not answer her until tomorrow anyway, and she needed guidance *now*.

Ira began to unlock her screen, but she decided against it. She actually didn't need advice. She was seeking permission to let herself go for once. She'd been the good one, the reliable one, not going to New York or LA to chase her dreams and passions. But at thirty-one years old, she didn't need permission. If she wanted a braless cuddle with a man she'd only truly started talking to that week, well then damn it, she would. And enjoy it. Without regrets.

The knock on the door made her bobble the phone in her hands, but she called an absent, "Come in!" as she stuffed the device back into her purse. Max entered wearing a blue tank top and black athletic shorts while carrying two glasses of water with paper towels underneath them to catch the condensation. A smile stretched across her face at his consideration;

unfortunately for him, she could see his cheeks redden in return.

"That's very thoughtful of you," she said, tilting her chin to one of the waters in his hand.

"I always have a glass of water before bed," he explained, setting one of the glasses on the nightstand. "Do you have a preference of which side of the bed?"

She shrugged. "I usually sleep on the left."

"I usually sleep by the door."

They were at a small impasse, then, because the left was the side closest to the door.

"You take the left," he said after a pause. "I'm in my home. Any side of the bed should be comfortable when you're home."

"That's a pretty philosophical thought," Ira said, grinning.

Max shrugged and took a sip of water from the glass he still held. "Yeah. Maybe one day it'll stick."

Her grin faded and she crossed her arms at her chest. "Max, if you prefer the left—"

He shook his head and gave her a soft smile. "Not at all. Besides, I'm more focused on sticking to you right now."

Shocked laughter burst from Ira, and she clapped her palm over her mouth. He grinned outright at her now, a naughty gleam in his eyes that had Ira sucking her teeth and nudging him with her shoulder as she passed by him to her side of the bed. "A CEO and a comedian, huh?"

"Gotta be multifaceted in this escort business," he whispered into her ear, his lips brushing against her lobe. He pulled away and went to his side of the bed, taking a long drink of water with a coy gaze in her direction. Ira snorted, rolling her eyes, and climbed into the bed. She took a sip of water from her glass.

"All right?"

"Yes, thanks," Ira replied, setting her glass back onto the nightstand before settling on her back. She stared at the high, smooth ceiling above her, different from the popcorn ceiling of her apartment.

"Ira."

She closed her eyes and took a deep breath before turning her head to face him. He still stood at the bed, his expression solemn.

"You're still okay with this?"

"Yes," she said, her eyes drifting along his muscular arms. "More than."

His lips curved. "Me too."

She watched him pull back the covers, watched him climb into bed, and watched him watch her expectantly.

"This feels unnatural, though," she said with a frown.

His eyebrows rose. "Okay?"

She shook her head with a scowl. "I mean, this is an arrangement, and I'm aware this is an arrangement. You wouldn't be doing this unless I'd asked."

He nodded as if that were obvious. "Consent is a big thing for me. The more explicitly and freely given, the better."

Ira couldn't argue that point, but, "This isn't romantic. It's clinical."

Now Max smiled. "Do you want it to be romantic?"

Ira didn't answer. When she'd said what she'd wanted, she'd only focused on the end result, not the getting there. Perhaps she should've indicated not only what she wanted, but *how* she wanted it. Yet, her voice got stuck on the words, an unexpected spate of tears coming forth instead.

Yes, she did. Ira wanted that, but she was afraid she wouldn't be able to let it go when the weekend was over. She'd talked a good game to herself earlier, but Monday was a specter now that the cuddling was about to begin. Looking at Max, at his willingness to give her what she sought, she could already feel herself becoming addicted and she hadn't even sampled the offering yet. This wasn't the first time she wished she were like Gideon, able to be capricious and indulge in flings of the heart for the immediate satiation of the body. For her job as a model, it was important for Gideon to make those quick, authentic connections and then break them once the shot was gotten. For Ira, once her heart was in it, it was in it—that was why she was so careful.

And yet, here was this man who, only after a few days, was easing the organ from her vice grip like it was nothing. Her brain was no match for the pull either. Knowing this was Max's job, knowing this was how Max had garnered his wealth, couldn't stop the transfer. It would be the height of silly for her to think he was feeling similar to her, but her heart had taken over perception.

Ira closed her eyes and gathered her courage. She might be inexperienced in relationships, but she recognized the look of a man who liked what he saw and wanted to know more.

Maybe she could *learn* him a thing or several.

Six

M ax was not a stranger to the wealth of feelings clients experienced during Dream Dates. He'd held more women, dried more tears, soothed more hurts and disappointments than he could count. But watching Ira navigate whatever emotional tumult to the resolve that now settled upon her features without his active aid astounded him.

He also didn't like it. Not because he was selfish enough to want that glory for himself, but rather because it showed she was too adept at holding herself together. She'd probably had more cracks rend her walls tonight than she'd had in years, and she'd admitted she wasn't used to physical affection.

A damn hug for her birthday. That was ri-*fucking*-diculous. And a little too close to home.

Ira Jackson was not a singular client. She was one of a number who were similar in reluctance and who analyzed what this Date experience could mean for them after the money was exchanged and goodbyes were said. Max didn't bother trying to figure out the source because usually, the women were trying to get *away* from it. And figuring out that puzzle meant emotional investment, and emotional investment was anathema in this line of work.

Ira Jackson was worth the entirety of his life savings.

Max's eyes opened at her touch. He hadn't even realized he'd closed them, but he supposed the detonation of that truth bomb caused such a reflexive response. Her palm was soft and warm against his jaw. He tilted his hand to brush his lips against the heel of her palm, but to do anything else would be absurd. Her fingers teased his left sideburn and he shivered at her gentle touch, his eyes closing again.

"I want it romantic," Ira whispered. "I want tenderness and romance, and to give them as much as receive them."

Oh, Holy Jesus, he wanted them too—every drop of affection she could spare.

His eyes still closed, Max brought the center of her palm to his lips with both of his hands. He pressed a long kiss upon her head line, swaying with the mattress as she shifted closer to him. His mouth dragged down to her wrist, feeling the rapid pulse underneath the delicate skin, and smiled as her fingers combed through the curls upon his forehead.

"These glasses though . . ."

He laughed now and shrugged. "They're staying on until I go to sleep because I don't want to miss a second of you."

She giggled, which had the unwelcome effect of removing her hand from his person so she could cover her mouth. Max growled his dismay and buried his face into her neck. She still smelled like pineapples, and he moaned. She gasped and whimpered, stretching out next to him and bucking her hips into the air.

"Max . . ."

His name on her sigh made him twitch in his shorts. He'd heard it cloaked in arousal before, and yet this was the first time in a long while that he couldn't ignore his own reaction in favor of hers. His body acknowledged the woman beside him was too profound to be a client. She'd tapped into something he'd long thought would remain locked forever.

"Ira," he murmured, letting his lips caress her skin with the shape of her name. She shivered and stretched her arm about his stomach to draw him closer. He ended up draping her right side, though he was mindful not to put too much of his weight on her. He pulled back and cupped her cheek, thrilled by her blown pupils and swollen bottom lip that she must've been biting.

"Good?" he asked.

"Yeah. You?"

He drew closer to her face and drifted the backs of his fingers along her dark cheek. "Good. I really want to kiss you now."

She smiled sheepishly, scrunching her nose, and it was such a precious sight to him. "I'm incredibly out of practice, just a warning."

"I'll be more than happy to get you back up to speed," he whispered, touching his nose to hers. She was so soft and pliant underneath him. Her body was the best kind of aphrodisiac, and he couldn't stop himself from squeezing her ample hips in his hands. She quivered and giggled again, making him smile in response.

"A kiss and sleep," she recalled, framing his face in her hands. "And suddenly, I ain't too sleepy."

Max hummed his approval at her words and kissed her upper lip, grinning at her disappointed mew. She wriggled underneath him and spread her legs, and he could do nothing but settle his hips into the cradle of her plush thighs. It took everything not to grind into her heat; there was no hiding his arousal. It was amazing how much he'd missed his libido until he'd discovered it again.

Max relished the give and spring of Ira's body. He was aware of how his hands trembled as they drifted along her form, curving over the generous dips and valleys she possessed. Her stomach was one of his favorite destinations. It was round like a dome and quivered with sensitivity to his light touch. He didn't delve underneath her clothes though he wanted to see if she were as soft everywhere else as she was on her arms and neck and face. He suspected so, but confirmation of it would be welcome too.

Throughout all of this, Max nibbled and tugged on her upper lip, keeping her the recipient and him the giver. This was part one of her boons, after all, and he didn't want to overwhelm her too much. He felt the unpracticed, mistimed purses of her mouth underneath his, the unsure squeezes of her hands upon his arms as if trying to find the right placement and pressure with which to hold him. He wanted to ask how long it'd been, if she were so unused to a hug and a kiss that they were relegated to birthday gifts. Yet he recalled her brilliant eyes and her rough reaction when he'd teased her about Sleeping Beauty. He knew well that the sound of a laugh was different when it came from a place of pain instead of joy. That was how he'd laughed for the majority of his childhood. Even now, he was more familiar with that sound even though he had much more pleasure in his life.

Ira was a pleasure, too, one he didn't want to think about relinquishing in three days, so he gathered her closer and kissed her harder, though only just. He groaned softly when she cradled his face in her hands, felt his heart swell with the tenderness she gave and the curious return presses of her lips against his. He opened his mouth upon hers but kept his tongue in check, enveloping her full lips to suck on them, trying to draw the mint toothpaste from her mouth and the pineapple sweetness he'd scented upon her. She chuckled throatily, moving her hands to his neck to twist her fingers in his dark-brown curls.

He smiled as he ended their kiss. "You like my hair."

"I like more than that," she said, her voice deeper, syrupier than before.

He nipped at the rounded point of her nose and laughed when she scrunched her face. "What else?"

She shrugged, now smoothing her palms down his back to his flanks. "I like you're big all over."

"I used to play football," he said. "Linebacker. I could've gone to the draft, but I wasn't passionate enough to give it my body for the next decade—if I were lucky."

Ira nodded. She was caressing his sides now, and she had no qualms about going underneath his tank top. Max hummed and grabbed a healthy thigh to drape around his hip. His erection pressed more into her center, making her hiss and him sigh.

"I like you all over, too, Ira Jackson," Max said, stroking the back of her thigh from her raised knee to the glorious curve of her ass. Her small smile became a beam, so much so her eyes crinkled at the corners. He smiled as well, dropping his forehead to hers.

"You like the fact I'm *big* all over?" Ira asked, though it was more teasing than fishing.

"Oh, I do like me a whole lotta woman," Max assured, squeezing her love handles affectionately. "I like the feel of you underneath me very much. I think I'd like the feel of you on top of me too."

"Can you stay where you are, though?" she asked, pausing her strokes at his sides. "I really like the weight of you."

He nodded, then asked, "Can I make a quick adjustment?"

She looked bemused, yet curious, and eventually nodded. He pressed a quick kiss to her cheek then slid down her body until his cheek lay against her chest. He felt the quiet power of her laugh vibrate underneath him and he didn't bother stopping his happy sigh when her arms closed about him.

"Do you want me to kiss the top of your head too?" she asked.

He snuggled into her softness. "I'm game."

She snickered above him, but the kiss came to the crown of his head anyway, and he smiled.

"Again . . . the *glasses*."

Max huffed, not nearly inclined to move, but he did lift his head just enough to take off the glasses before he reached across her to set them on her nightstand. She eyed him but he ignored it, burrowing back into the generous mounds of her breasts while draping his arm about her belly. Their legs tangled together, and

Ira began a steady pass of her fingers through his hair. He became drowsy, his blurry vision hiding behind the darkness of his eyelids.

"Are you fallin' asleep?" she asked, her voice still thick and slow.

"You're so soothing," he said by way of answer. "Soft and soothing."

He began to nuzzle her left breast with his nose, letting the point graze her nipple. It hardened beneath the shirt, a small pebble he wanted to lick and mouth. His tongue became heavy with the desire, so he pressed it hard against his teeth. This cuddle session would become something else entirely if he gave into temptation.

"Glad I could be of service," she murmured against his crown.

He sighed deeply. "I'm supposed to be servicing *you*." He stroked her belly from her waist to the underside of her breast and back. He could not stop touching her, caressing her.

"You are," she promised. "A kiss and a cuddle and a hold throughout the night. I've gotten the kiss, we're doin' the cuddle, and the sleepin' is upon us."

She said the last part on a yawn, which made him yawn and close his eyes. He didn't bother opening them again as he continued to speak.

"I hope the kissing wasn't just for tonight."

"No," she said, tugging his hair playfully. "Them lips are mine until I leave."

He smiled. "All of me is yours," he corrected unthinkingly, but he didn't call the words back. A peace settled upon him at that statement, making his limbs heavy enough to sink into Ira with complete abandon.

Max did not mean just until Monday.

Seven

I ra woke up on her birthday with a hand clutching her breast and an erection tucked against her ass. Max snored behind her, his chin atop her head since she'd become a piece of the puzzle he'd created with their bodies. He'd fallen asleep on her last night—literally—and it'd been all well and good until she couldn't draw a proper breath once slumber had taken a firm hold of him. He'd whined and grumbled like a toddler when she'd roused him enough to get him off her; but once he'd settled on his side of the bed, he'd pulled her back immediately to his front and had recommenced his soft snores.

All in all, the "sleep" portion of her gift had gone rather well.

Her ears twitched as she recognized the sound that had awakened her in the first place. The drone of her phone's vibrating in her purse clear across the room irritated Ira, but no one would call this early unless something was incredibly wrong.

The arm around her tightened when she started to move.

"Stay. I'll get it."

Max's voice was the height of rudeness early in the morning with its deep rumble, as were his soft, yet dry lips pressing a kiss underneath her earlobe. Ira shifted onto her back once he left the bed, reclining against the headboard, and got an eyeful of his tight behind walking toward the chair in the corner where her purse was. After a moment's search, he returned with a disappointed expression on his face while handing her the quiet phone.

"Murphy?"

Ira smiled. "My younger sister. She's in Europe, so the early call makes sense. I'm sorry for it, though."

He shrugged, bracketing her body with his arms before bending down to kiss her lips sweetly. "As wrong as this may be, I'm glad I still get to be the one to wish you a happy birthday first."

Ira laughed and accepted his mouth again. Like last night, Max nibbled and tugged on her lips, keeping things light and playful. She grasped his shirt at his hips and brought him closer until she was lying on the bed, and he hovered above. She jumped when she felt her phone vibrate again at her hip, and Max chuckled with one final tug on her upper lip before pulling away.

"Your sister again?" She checked the screen and nodded. "I'll let y'all talk in private."

He kissed her forehead softly before leaving. "Happy birthday, Ira."

She answered the call, glad they weren't on video because her cheesing smile would've cracked the screen. "What time is it over there?"

"Oh, snap! Girl, I'm sorry!" Murphy immediately replied. "I was leaving you a message and I accidentally ended the call before I was finished. I didn't even think—what time is it where you are?"

Ira could hear music start and stop in the background as she told her sister the time. "Are you about to perform?"

"We're in sound check; we perform tonight at six," Murphy clarified. "These Europeans love themselves some jazz, girl. It's been wild, but fun!"

Murphy was the primary pianist and arranger for Sasha Lorne, an award-winning jazz vocalist. Given her success with Sasha, including a Grammy nomination, Ira was glad she'd insisted Murphy answer Sasha's call instead of celebrating her thirtieth birthday last year. Hopefully, Ira would have plenty more birthdays to come, but once-in-a-lifetime opportunities were just that. One should take them when they appeared.

Ira looked around at the Miami condo guestroom and chuckled to herself. Take them, indeed. "I'm so glad you're having a great time."

"Yeah, but I wish I could be spending it with you too," Murphy said. "But I knew it was early so I wanted to try to get you your birthday song to wake up to, but I messed it up. I thought I'd dodged a bullet when you didn't answer but of course you'd be awake early in the morning. On a Saturday. On your birthday."

Ira grinned and shrugged. "It's all right. It's been a great birthday morning so far. I love you."

"I love you!" Murphy chirped back. "I wish I'd had enough money to fly you out here, but I'm not at that level yet. Goals, though."

"I know. Of that I have no doubt," Ira said sincerely. It would only be a matter of time. Murphy was built like her, more curves than the popular music scene preferred. Yet as visually dependent as the music business was, talent was still talent, and Murphy overflowed with it.

They caught up with each other because usually Ira was at work when Murphy could talk or vice versa. Murphy then sang her original song she'd written for Ira, which was the most ridiculous song she'd ever heard in her life and just what she'd needed to hear. The effect wasn't as great as it could've been because Murphy couldn't sing a bad note if she tried (and she had—no dice), but her overcompensation was so hilarious Ira began that clicking laugh one did when lungs couldn't get enough air.

"I want in on the joke."

Ira ignored Murphy's audible gasp and covered the speaker of her phone with her hand. "No joke, not really. What's up?"

"Wanted to know if you drank coffee," Max said. "Or if you'd prefer tea."

"What kind of tea?"

"Green," he replied.

"That's perfect, thank you."

Max nodded and left. Murphy was keening in her ear, sounding like a boiling kettle.

"Wayment, is that Gideon's friend? Did you—!"

"*No*," Ira said stressed, but she couldn't keep the impishness out of her voice. "Not yet anyway."

"Girl, *what!* You're actually thinking about it!" Murphy squealed and Ira chuckled. "I didn't think you would! I can't believe you are!"

"I can't either," Ira agreed. "But I'm taking this chance and I'm enjoying myself so far."

"I'll bet!" Murphy said with a laugh. "You really think you're ready to *finally* pop your cherry?"

Ira shrugged. "Maybe? I mean, I did think I'd wait for marriage, but I think that was more me not wanting to disappoint Aunt Dot and not what I truly thought. Up until now, it'd been a moot point because there had never been mutual interest."

"And you think there is now?"

"Yes," she said, and the word was as thrilling as it was scary. Even if a huge motivation of Max's interest was manufactured because of the role he was playing, hers was still there and unignorable.

"Girl, I heard that man's voice over the phone and it sounded like sex. Who knew a white boy could sound like that? He sounds like a brotha."

Ira snorted. "It's a nice voice. Pure torture early in the morning, though."

"I'm sure!" Murphy laughed. "So, you've chosen Gideon's friend for the date? I don't know why I'm surprised you decided to go with a white guy."

"I've dated all kinds of guys in the past." Ira shrugged. "And really, there's already a level of trust there *because* he's Gideon's friend. I trust her judgment. It wasn't supposed to be him initially, but then he suggested I come down so he can help me decide and . . . well . . . he has."

There was a pause filled with nothing but "Mic check one, two, three" on repeat four times before Murphy could find her voice again.

"That's fair. As long as a person treats you right and with respect, that's all I care about."

Ira nodded, then shrugged even though Murphy couldn't see her. "Besides, I might not even have my partnered sexual debut, so this all might be a premature conversation."

"This conversation's never premature," Murphy assured. "Have sex because *you want it* for whatever reasons that make sense to *you*. Whatever that *something* is you need to make this step, don't go for it without it."

"And what if now after thirty-one years of life, I've finally found that something in this most random of circumstances?" Ira asked skeptically.

"Well, hell, good that you finally found it! I'm glad you waited until *you* were ready and not because of whatever bullshit societal timetable folk follow so they won't seem 'weird.' I wish I'd done that."

At that moment, Ira wished she were in Brussels so she could hug her sister tightly. She still hadn't gotten the full story of the first—and only—relationship Murphy had ever been in, but Ira knew it hadn't ended well and she wasn't sure if it'd begun any better.

"You have good instincts, Ira," Murphy finally continued. "It's okay to trust them. I'm lettin' myself trust this guy and I've not even met him yet, simply because you like him."

"He's Gideon's friend. She gave him my number."

Murphy snorted, but then she hummed thoughtfully. "Do you think she was actually matchmaking on the sly for you?"

Ira had to smile. "I wouldn't put it past her. She'd talk so much about how she'd 'almost' introduce me to this person or that but never did. So why Max? Why make sure we connected at her birthday party? In fact, I think he was the only person she insisted I have his number."

"Why anyone?" Murphy asked. "Not that I'm a firm believer in 'one true love,' but I do believe there are people on this earth who were meant to be in our lives. Some we'll never meet and some we're lucky enough to meet. We don't know for how long or in what way, but maybe Max is one of those people for you. The meeting is the easy part. The courage to follow through is really what makes the difference."

Ira severely wanted to ask if her sister were talking from personal experience, but then Murphy spoke again.

"I gotta jet. It's our sound check slot. I love you, happy birthday, and I hope there are filthy details to be had come Monday, and I'll want *all of* them. I'll stop playing a set just so I can hear them, I swear!"

Ira laughed and hugged herself since she couldn't hug her sister. "I love you. Be epic tonight!"

"Always am, girl!"

The call ended and Ira didn't bother putting her phone back in her purse. The accessory was across the room still and the bed was entirely too comfortable. Instead, she let her sister's words settle inside of her. Though she'd told herself she hadn't needed any advice, Ira definitely appreciated her sister's insights. She would trust her instincts. Trust the safety and familiarity Max engendered in her. Trust the libido that had suddenly roared to life upon the first sound of his voice, and which had only roared louder the longer she'd been in his presence.

Trust that she was also giving him something he'd been yearning to have despite his vast experience in the art of companionship. Out of all the women he'd escorted, befriended, and more, Ira couldn't imagine he'd clung to them the way he'd clung to her throughout the night. This was her instinct talking, to be sure; but there were levels of sincerity, different sources of impetus that influenced the action.

Max had needed last night just as much as she had.

She couldn't forget his tortured expression as he'd finished straightening up his kitchen last night. Her arms had ached to hug him, and she'd even wrapped her feet around the legs of the stool she'd sat on to keep herself put. There were boundaries to respect, and they didn't know each other enough for such intimacies. Nevertheless, they'd both wanted those intimacies all the same.

Last night had been a good start, a sufficient appetizer for the appetite she still had. At least the need didn't claw and twist and ache like it had. Now it was a hum, almost soothing, as it knew it could be slaked at some point.

Would.

Ira slipped out of bed and brushed her teeth before going downstairs, her phone in hand. Max was at the stove with a steaming mug at his right and a waffle iron on the counter behind him. A pan sizzled before him, white wisps of smoke curling into the exhaust fan above. He looked up at her entrance and frowned.

"You're out of bed."

"That a problem?" she asked, coming up to the island stove. She pointed at the mug, setting her phone down beside it. "That mine?"

"Yeah," he confirmed, still frowning. "I was gonna give you breakfast in it."

She smiled. "In bed? That's really sweet, but unnecessary. I didn't know you cooked."

He shrugged, his expression becoming more placid. "It's my best meal, though. Anything beyond some spaghetti and I'm useless."

"Impossible," she assured him, coming until she was right by his side. "I don't think you could ever be useless."

He smiled and paused from tending to the bacon he was frying to press a long kiss to her forehead. "Have a good talk with your sister?"

"Yes," she murmured, tugging him closer to her. "Another, please."

Humming quietly, Max kissed the bridge of her nose next. "Yeah?"

"Another."

He gave her a kiss on the tip of her nose. "Your tea?"

"You have a microwave," she said, touching their noses together. "Turn off the stove, Max, so you don't burn down this pretty condo."

Eight

Max's condo was safe from fire, but not his libido, when the loud buzz of Ira's vibrating phone on the glass countertop jarred them both out of their lust-filled haze. They glared at the offensive device, then smirked at each other when they saw the name on her screen.

Gids.

"Mind if I go out on the balcony?" she asked.

Max shook his head, looking out through those tall windows to see the gorgeous morning that hadn't even met its full bloom yet. "We can have breakfast out there if you'd like."

"I would," Ira said with a grin. "See you soon."

He almost let the bacon burn from watching her ass sway away.

Max was excited about being domestic for someone, not having had the chance to do it in a long time. When he'd first started escorting, this was one of the primary services he'd offered his clients. Some women had just wanted a day of pampering by a young, virile man, and breakfast in bed would be a fantasy of theirs. He'd even fed them bites from his fork or fingers (primarily fingers), and the feeding would become so erotic the plate would end up abandoned and the client would become the feast.

Max flitted his eyes to the window where Ira had sprawled into one of the patio chairs, thick legs hanging over the arms while her braless chest wiggled with the force of her laugh. The sun practically gleamed upon her dark skin, and her wide smile made him wish he were the cause and the recipient of it. She was so damn stunning to him; he'd love the chance to feast upon her.

The pungent smell of burnt pork made him scowl, and he yanked his eyes from Ira to the charred strips of bacon in his nonstick pan. He sighed and threw the ruined strips away, though his inattention amused him. There was something almost refreshing about being this gone over a woman. He felt his blood pumping anew and his body hummed with the prospect of being emotionally and sexually well fed. Honestly, he hadn't thought Ira would be down for any physical intimacies beyond hugs and maybe a few kisses when she'd come to Miami. His offer for her to stay here had been completely above board. He'd even started making calls to a few of his local Dudes yesterday trying to find one who would provide the perfect experience for her. Yet out of all of his fantastic employees, none of them had satisfied him as enough for her.

He snorted. As if *his* standards were the ones that mattered in this scenario.

Max put new uncooked strips of bacon in the frying pan before checking on the waffle batter he'd let sit for a few minutes by the waffle iron. He then went to the refrigerator and pulled out the fruit salad he'd prepared. It was a kaleidoscope of berries and melons, and he smiled softly when he spied a thick wedge of pineapple on top of the salad.

Ira still smelled like them even this morning.

He spied the mug she'd neglected to take out with her on the balcony and refreshed it. Once he removed the perfectly browned strips of bacon from the pan, he then took the mug and a small bowl of the fruit salad out to her, his heart squeezing at the bright smile of thanks she bestowed upon him.

"Max is a veritable *prince*," Ira drawled into the phone. He grinned, knowing this was for his benefit, but he appreciated the sentiment all the same. "He is serving at my pleasure and it's really nice. Ten out of ten, would recommend."

"How else is he 'serving your pleasure?'" Max heard Gideon ask suggestively. The phone was on speaker.

"Hugs and kisses," Ira said without missing a beat and he heard Gideon suck her teeth.

"That's it?" Gideon exclaimed, aghast. "That big ol' jungle gym of a man and you're just *huggin'* him? Ira—!"

Ira took the phone off speaker and placed the call on mute. "Oh, my goodness, I'm sorry!"

Max crouched down to her level and held out his hand for the phone. "Want me to talk to her?"

She peered at him for a moment. "Do *you*?"

Max started to shake his head, but then he nodded and waggled his fingers. "I'll talk to her."

Ira nodded, unmuting the phone and telling her cousin Max wanted to speak to her for a second.

"And could you bring some honey if you have some?" Ira asked once he stood after taking her phone.

"She talkin' 'bout the kind in the bottle, right?" Gideon asked in his ear.

Max nodded his assent to Ira but didn't reply to Gideon until he was back in the kitchen.

"*Was* the reason you gave me Ira's number for me to have sex with your cousin?"

"Well, hello to you too!" Gideon snipped. "And . . . not *exactly*."

Max groaned, going to his pantry to take out a jar of honey. "Gideon! When you gave me her number, I didn't think you meant *me* to be the one—"

"Oh, please!" Gideon interrupted. "I saw how you two looked at each other at my birthday party and I knew *both* of you wouldn't do anything about it unless I intervened!

That's why I told you to write your personal number on the back of your business card! That's why I gave you *hers* because I knew she wouldn't even think to do it! Besides, I know you'll be able to show my cousin a good time without completely freaking her out, all right? I've seen you charm the coldest of women at networking functions, Max; and while Ira isn't frigid, the woman has never had a warm touch that wasn't hers!"

Max paused at the insinuation, his eyebrows gathering together. "What are you talkin' about?"

Gideon gasped sharply, then cursed. "Never mind about that, Max."

Max clamped his mouth shut, determined to keep his curiosity at bay. He had an inkling of what she meant, but that wasn't Gideon's business to tell nor his to know until Ira wanted to tell him . . . *if* she wanted to tell him.

"The point is," Gideon marched on, "as much as I'm all about Dream Dude LLC, I'm only trusting my cousin with someone I know who'd do his best to show her a good time. Not just because there's a paycheck involved, but because it's your mission to make a woman feel like a queen for a day . . . or a weekend, as apparently is the case. You're not charging Ira for this, are you?"

Max rolled his eyes and didn't dignify the question with a response, going back outside to give Ira her honey. She smiled her thanks around a bite of melon then frowned at his displeased expression.

"What's wrong?" she asked after she swallowed.

He shook his head and handed her back the phone. "Waffles will be ready in five."

Max tried very hard to focus solely on making the waffles and not on the kernel of suspicion growing in his mind. Yet as much as he tried not to be, he remained fixated on Gideon's almost confession and tried to map that with the other clues gleaned from previous conversations. Ira had admitted she hadn't been on a date in a while, and that little jump she'd given when he'd put his hands on her waist had been something he'd bookmarked in his mind. He'd given her the out of being ticklish, but she hadn't fully taken it. And then there had been the awkwardness of those initial kisses . . . there was out of practice and then there was *never had been*.

"No," he muttered to himself, filling two glasses with water. He refused to believe she hadn't been kissed at all. She'd certainly taken to it like a fish to water after those first few awkward moments, and kissing wasn't just like riding a bike. Each one was a new experience, with new textures and flavors to be discovered.

He licked his lips, remembering the minty freshness of her mouth last night, and wondered if her mouth tasted of berries now thanks to the fruit salad she'd been eating. Maybe she actually tasted like pineapples too.

Breakfast went by with little dialogue, both deciding to enjoy the warm breeze and the wonderful breakfast.

He kept looking at her, however, and she kept ignoring him, her focus on Biscayne Bay before them. Max didn't mind the silence even if it were tenser than he preferred, at least on his part. Ira seemed more contemplative than anything else, and he wondered what she and Gideon had discussed before they ended the call.

"This was so good. Thank you, Max," Ira said after she finished her last bite of waffle.

He smiled and nodded. "You're welcome. Gave me an opportunity to shake off some rust."

She smiled and sipped her tea. "I understand that. I don't cook as often as I should. It's not so much fun when it's a meal for one."

Max nodded again, still regarding her closely. He'd learned better than to assume every woman wanted a spouse and a gaggle of kids at her feet. Just because a woman was a natural nurturer didn't mean she wanted to be a wife and mother. Maybe he was placing his own wishes and wistfulness onto a person who didn't think similarly—all because he wanted *this* person to be that much more of a potential candidate for his own dream fulfillment.

He looked away from her and stood abruptly, clenching his hands into fists to hide their trembling.

"What's wrong?" Ira asked, quickly standing herself. She looked around frantically. "You saw a bug or something?"

He had to snicker. "I thought you guys lived in the country. That's what Gideon said."

Ira made a face. "Like we had a choice in that! And just because we did, that don't mean bugs and I were *friends*! Boy, if you don't get!"

He laughed more, grateful for the break and the spotlight being jerked away from him. He didn't tease her about her reaction, however, and instead grabbed their now-empty plates. "You're welcome to stay out here . . . make some new friends with six-to-eight–legged creatures while I clean these dishes."

She sucked her teeth and glared at him. "You play *entirely* too much, Max!"

He gave her a wide berth as she snatched up her fruit bowl and glass before marching into the condo, the effect dampened when she had to reorganize her load to get a good grip on the patio door's handle. He let all of his chuckles out while he stacked the teacup and saucer on the plates and cradled his water glass in his elbow so he, too, could enter the condo. The stream of water running at a fast clip reached his ears and he tsked loudly upon entering the kitchen.

"I thought chores were a no-no this weekend," he chastised gently, setting his own dirty armful on the counter.

"Max, it makes no sense to let these dishes sit in the sink when I, at the *very* least, can load them in the dishwasher," Ira said, not even pausing her scrubbing of the frying pan. He stared at her until she looked up at him, then glanced meaningfully at her sudsy hands and pan, and smirked when she looked at him dead in the eyes and continued to clean.

"That's the last dish you wash, Miss Jackson," Max declared. "Or I'm takin' you over my knee."

"Kinky."

A surprised laugh bubbled forth. "You like to be spanked?"

Ira shrugged. "I didn't like it as a child, but adults always have new perspectives on things."

That was not a no. Max bit his bottom lip, his eyes dropping down to the generous body part she possessed. He hadn't become acquainted with it nearly enough last night, her sides and belly taking up the majority of his interest. Nevertheless, he kept his hands to himself and started putting his dishes in the left sink; she was occupying the right one.

"Is this a not-so-subtle attempt for me to stop?"

He grinned and shrugged. "I can't risk the spanking. You might like it."

She scrunched up her face against the laugh he could tell she wanted to let out, but she won that battle with a guttural sigh and stepped away from the sink.

"You really don't want me to help?"

"Dates don't generally help."

"I'm not a general date," she returned, tilting her head to the side. "The sooner we get this done, the sooner we can do 'funner' things." She made air quotes with sudsy fingers to emphasize the nontraditional word.

"Fine," Max conceded. "What are the 'funner' things you want to do?"

"I don't know!" Ira said, laughing, "but watching you do chores ain't too high on the list, bruh!"

That was a solid point, but, "I can dance while I wash."

Her eyes brightened and so did her smile. "You gon' *Magic Mike* it for me?"

He smirked at her and then did a body roll that made her eyes darken. Oh, yes, he had some moves.

Ira squealed with a verve of a girl half her age and rushed out the kitchen. "Gettin' my phone!" Max grinned, excited to do this for her since he didn't feel like he had to *perform* so much as to have fun and let Ira enjoy it. He'd finished rinsing off the abandoned frying pan and placed it in the stainless-steel dish rack when she returned, and she queued up the music for him. Ginuwine's "Pony" began to play, because *of course it did.*

"Oldie but a goodie, huh?" Max commented.

"Yes. Bust them moves, Worthington!"

He definitely put on a show, doing his best barre routines from his old college days when he'd taken ballet lessons to help with his core strength and balance for football . . . and to get close to a ballerina who'd been in his Finance class. Lots of pliés with booty bounces and more body rolls and pelvic thrusts. Her giggles and whoops rained on him like dollar bills at the club and were far more valuable. He even used the sprayer to add to the effect, rinsing his dishes with far more drama and water than was required. By the time the dishes were in the dishwasher, his shirt and the floor were good and soaked. "Slow Motion" by Juvenile now played from Ira's phone.

Ira clapped her approval of his performance as she stood. "Where's your mop, *Mike*?"

He grinned and rolled his eyes. "Hall closet. I'll get—"

"Stay put," she ordered. "No need to track that water everywhere."

He did, peeling off his sodden tank top and setting it on the counter before taking a long sheet of paper towels to begin drying the floor. He was glad he'd opted for his contacts today; the last thing he wanted to deal with was streaky glasses.

"Waste, waste, waste in our haste!" Ira chastised, bringing the mop into the kitchen. Max stood from his crouched position, his nipples and cock hardening at the roam of her eyes down his body. His dick danced when her eyes made a pit stop at his crotch, and he moaned when that full bottom lip of hers disappeared between her teeth.

"Ira," he gruffly muttered, and those dark-brown eyes hastily jerked to his green ones before squeezing shut.

"I'm sorry," she apologized, thrusting the mop to him while turning her face away. "That was rude of me."

It hadn't felt rude to *him*. In fact, he'd gotten harder at her obvious appreciation of his arousal, and he'd wanted nothing more in the world than for her to touch him, to put those full lips around him and bring him to his pleasure. And though this weekend wasn't about him, it *was* about *her*, and he had a sneaking suspicion their wants and desires were perfectly aligned.

"It's okay," Max assured her, approaching her carefully until they were toe to toe. He could see the small shudder of her body and heard her rough exhalation. He needed Ira to look at him, to see he was *more* than okay that she found him attractive.

"Ira," he whispered again, taking the mop's handle and setting the implement aside against the counter before bringing her carefully against him. She burrowed her hips unconsciously against his and he moaned softly, his breath catching when those soft hands of hers settled upon his chest.

"Max?"

"Yeah?"

"I'm wet."

He groaned and buried his face into her neck. He was going to die, and Ira was going to kill him. What a hell of a way to go.

Nine

Honest to goodness, Ira had meant *literally* wet, as Max's chest was still damp, but the direction his mind had obviously gone in wasn't incorrect either. Watching him dance hadn't left her unaffected, but now that she was in his arms, she was starting to be as soaked as the floor still was.

His kisses were hot and humid at the curve of her neck, and her nipples hardened beneath the T-shirt she wore. She could feel the acceleration of his heartbeat underneath her palm, and the slight undulation of his hips against hers made her whimper.

"You're wet," he muttered against her skin. "Did I make you wet?"

She crowded close to him. The pain of her sensitive nipples pressed against him was also pleasurable and she rocked against him unwittingly. "Yeah." Innocently or no, he *had*.

He smoothed his hands down her sides until they settled on her hips to still her. "Will you let me see?" To underscore the question, thick digits snuck beneath the waistband of her yoga pants but went no farther than that. His light touch scalded her skin even though she shivered in response, and she clenched her thighs together. She could feel herself dripping now.

"Max," she gasped, sliding her hands up his chest to grip his shoulders. Ira rested her forehead against his temple and released a long sigh as his fingers began a caress. She'd not felt another's touch upon her body like this and was arrested with the indecision of what to do, how to feel. Ira was usually so protective of her personal space, and Max had been able to breach it with little effort. He'd disarmed her so smoothly, leaving her feeling exposed in a way she hadn't realized she'd clamored to experience. There was a freedom in such abject vulnerability; and maybe because he made a living in doing this, that he had experience and knew not to take such a thing for granted, that Ira allowed herself full rein to experience it too.

He'd guaranteed they'd go no further than she allowed. He wouldn't pressure her . . . wouldn't *judge* her.

That was the real kicker, Ira realized. Dating was always so fraught with judgment and snap decisions that could have long-lasting ramifications. Whatever happened here only existed within the terms of their agreed-upon time with the knowledge one might not come out completely unscathed. Ira very much feared she might become addicted to Max's touch in a way she hadn't anticipated. There was a veritable pool between her legs and his fingers hadn't even drifted below her belly button yet.

But they *were* stroking the hell out of her stomach, the soft, fleshy mass magazines and commercials said should be tight and flat to live one's best life. Truthfully, she *liked* her stomach; would often play with it in the mirror and giggle as it jiggled and rippled. Granted, it'd taken her some time to get to where she was, but the decision to love herself had been among the best she'd ever made and also among the most liberating. That hadn't meant it'd been easy to find someone who could love her as much as she did, because lust and fetish were not the same, not to mention aligned minds and spirits. And truthfully, her alone had felt so good these last few years she hadn't been too pressed to find a partner to share it with her.

"Still with me?"

Ira blinked her eyes open, shocked that she'd been sagging against Max so completely and so lost in her own thoughts. He was still caressing her, but the touch had turned from arousing to comforting. She didn't know who was being comforted, however. Max's tone had lost that gruff edge and was now indulgent and drowsy.

"Clearly," she cracked, snuggling into him. Her breasts flattened against his hard chest, and she wrapped her arms around his neck. "I love your touch."

Max chuckled deeply in his throat, making his chest rumble. She loved the sensation. "I love to touch you."

"Can I touch you too?"

Max turned his head, brushing the sharp point of his nose against the rounded one of hers before bringing their lips together. "*Please.*"

Shuddering at the bald yearning in his voice, Ira splayed her hand along the ridges of his abdomen, grinning a little when the muscles jumped underneath her palm. He still continued his strokes, but they went farther south with every pass. She didn't stop him, understanding he was asking her consent with each caress, and she was granting it to him. Ira didn't want to break the moment with words. Besides, Changing Faces' "Stroke You Up" was singing everything that needed to be said from her phone.

"How's your skin so soft," he asked against her lips. His breath was sweet from the fruit and maple syrup. "What do you use?"

"Shea butter," she murmured, her hand now slipping beneath the waistband of his shorts. She felt the crisp hair of his lower abdomen and her fingers twitched. So did his cock. The head of it brushed against the heel of her palm and she shuddered.

Then her head snapped back, her jaw dropping. "*Really*?"

He frowned in confusion and slight displeasure that she'd removed her face from kissing range. "What?"

She flexed her wrist, letting the heel of her hand drag purposefully along the tip of his erection, and his reddening face made a giggle bubble forth from her unexpectedly.

"It's . . . served me well."

"But, like, *where does it all go*?"

Max laughed and pressed a kiss to the hinge of her jaw. "Inside of you hopefully."

Ira was not going to survive the weekend.

"Is that okay?" he asked, now gripping her hips to align their pelvises. "Do you mind if I slide inside of you? Would you like me to? My fingers, my tongue, my cock? I can feel you tremblin', darlin'. Are you about to come for me? Just from this?"

Her pussy clenched, wishing his fingers *were* inside and not still drifting along her belly. Nevertheless, his words gave her the courage to grip him, and his low groan had her whimpering into the base of his neck. He was silky and pulsing in her palm, living steel. Her pussy clenched harder, wanting this inside of her, the torrent of lust unfamiliar yet not unwelcome.

"Grip me tighter," he whispered against the bridge of her nose. "Fuck, Ira, your hand. Shape me like you would your clay."

"You're too hard," she told him, but she did tighten her hold as she began to stroke. He sagged, forcing her to brace more of his weight, but he wasn't a burden. She tilted up her head and licked his lips slowly, at the same cadence with which she stroked his cock. However, he turned the tables when she felt his thick digits on her mound.

He groaned roughly. "Natural. Fuck."

"That bad?" Ira didn't shave. She was too lazy, and no one was seeing her anyway. She hadn't been presumptive enough to think anything like *this* would happen either.

He rested his forehead against hers and breathed harshly through his nose. "No." His fingers slid lower to where her cleft parted, and the sound of her damp lips separating seemed even louder than Silk's "Freak Me" that now played. Ira hissed in a sharp breath, gripping his neck tighter so she could remain standing, squeezing his cock roughly at the large shot of pleasure she'd experienced.

"You're close?" he asked, tugging her bottom lip gently. "I'm close. Your hand, baby, *damn*. I'm so hard I hurt. I wanna be inside you."

"In my mouth?" Her voice was a breathy whisper, and Max's deep whimper made her keen in response.

She'd never given a blowjob before, but her tongue felt heavy with the desire to try. She trusted Max to instruct her, help her learn how to give pleasure without harsh critique.

He gulped in a breath, his big body brushing against hers. "Ira."

The yearning in his voice had her dropping to her knees, the weight of his combined with hers too much for her to take. His growl of protest sent a fresh wave of arousal to her center, but she looked up at him with eager, coy eyes as she curled her fingers into the waistband of his shorts. The head of his cock peeked out and her tongue tingled with the need to wrap around it.

"You don't have to," he said, his voice sandpaper rough, his eyes glassy with lust.

"I wouldn't be down here if I didn't want to," she said, tugging the waistband but not pulling it down. "Do *you* want me to?"

He licked his lips and closed his eyes hard, shaking his head. "It's your birthday. I shouldn't—"

She kissed his bare flank, letting her tongue take a swipe at him, and she sighed against him when his hand found the top of her head.

"Please, Max," she whispered, splaying her hands along his firm sides, her eyes locked with his. "I want to learn."

His brows furrowed, and Ira waited on bated breath for his reply. She prayed fervently he wouldn't ask her what she'd meant or, more importantly, why she was even learning *now*. She hid her face, a sudden, sharp spike of embarrassment shoving away a great portion of her arousal. Thirty-one years old and she'd never had a cock in her mouth that wasn't plastic. Wasn't that just the peak of pathetic?

Gentle hands cupped her chin, drawing her face up so her eyes met his. His thumb stroked the fullness of her lips reverently, and her heart swelled.

"Start gently," he said quietly. "Just your lips and tongue on the tip first."

Her smile was automatic, mainly of relief with a healthy mix of excitement. The swing from one emotion to the next almost made her dizzy, but she carefully peeled the shorts down and gasped at the sight of his erection hard and proud against his belly. She'd watched her fair share of porn—she wouldn't deny that—but Max had one of the prettiest cocks she'd ever seen. There was a prominent blue vein that twisted and curled along the length, and she let her tongue travel the route on the way to the crown of his erection.

"Fuck."

Her pussy throbbed at the intoned expletive. He tasted of salt and tang, and the tip of him was softer than she'd anticipated. Max gripped her chin but not hard, not even guiding her. It was as if he needed her to ground himself in the moment, in the sensations she was creating inside of him. A thrill of power swirled inside of her.

She let her breath fan against the tip of him before closing her mouth along his head, careful to make sure her teeth didn't catch him too hard. She focused on the notch at the underside of the head with the point of her tongue, grinning when he jerked and grunted in response.

"Stroke me, darlin'," he managed to rasp. "Oh, fuckin' hell."

She stroked him a few times, her tongue dancing along the tip of him as she did. Her free hand found its way inside of her yoga pants beneath her panties. There was a small swamp in the crotch of her underwear, her center hot and gooey with the evidence of her arousal. She found her clit and began to stroke. It wasn't coordinated by any means, however. The majority of her focus was on his pleasure.

Sometimes she'd suck the head and stroke him, and he'd stand on his tiptoes and grunt for her to wait. She would for him, but not for herself. She was too close to her orgasm, and she hoped it'd be glorious instead of its usual whimper of defeat.

"Ira," he rasped, his hand back on the top of her head. "I'm close."

The words compelled her to be bold, so she took more of his length into her mouth, making her tongue bowl-like to accommodate his girth as well. She couldn't swallow him very far, her gag reflexes too strong, and saliva pooled into her mouth and dripped down her chin to her shirt. It was messy, inelegant, and raw. He began to thrust, as if he thought he could breach her reflex, but not too hard. They were little pulses meant to coax her mouth to relax, but she was strung too tightly for that to happen. So was he.

Someone had to give.

Ira pulled her mouth from him to kiss his length, starting at the base and working her way up to the head. Max fell back against the counter, his legs widening so she could move even closer. She gripped the sides of his hips while she sucked his balls. They were heavy and drawn. She knew enough to understand he really was close.

"You're gonna come, aren't you?" she murmured against his left iliac crest.

"Yes," he rasped. "Ira, darlin', *soon*."

She took the tip back into her mouth and sucked, drawing his orgasm to the surface. His body twitched and she instinctively pulled back in time for the first spurt to hit her cheek. She adjusted his cock so the rest of his release hit her chest and she stroked him through it, peppering kisses along his belly and hips until the tension in his body eased.

She rested her forehead against his stomach in the aftermath, their harsh breathing mingling with Ginuwine's "So Anxious" that now played. His climax took the edge off hers considerably, and she felt proud that her first foray into oral sex had gone so well.

"Ira?" Max asked after a moment. His voice was still frayed.

"Yeah?"

"I'm gonna make love to you."

Ira wasn't aware a heart could trip and squeeze at the same time, but hers did. "You don't have to. I didn't do that for sex. I did it because I wanted to, and I wanted you to enjoy it."

"Did you come?"

"No."

"I owe you an orgasm."

"This ain't a loan, Max. Yours was freely and enthusiastically given."

Strong hands suddenly cupped her face and he bent down, his mouth meeting hers. He made sure to stroke her tongue with his, and her body trembled with re-stoked arousal. By the time Max broke the kiss, Ira was on her feet again and his length was starting to firm up between them once more.

"Yours will be too," he promised against her lips.

Ten

I ra's cell phone rang, breaking the standoff between them. Max flagged the relief that had flitted across her face to discuss at a later time, and instead pulled up his shorts to cover his softening dick and grabbed the mop to clean up the kitchen floors. Ira answered the call in the living area. "Aunt Dot" was on the line and on speakerphone, but Ira's voice was overly flat, like she was trying to hide the fact her arousal was still thick and abundant inside of her.

It had to be, since that was how his lust felt inside of him still.

"Are you all right? You don't *sound* happy. I can assure you, dear, thirty-one isn't all that bad! In fact, by the time I was your age, I already had my law practice up and running *and* I had you four! I was just starting to live my full life. This is an exciting time, Ira, but don't let that daughter of mine get you into *too* much excitement. Is she around?"

Max perked up an eyebrow at the question. Gideon had mentioned once, briefly, that she and her mother weren't exactly on speaking terms, so it seemed Ira was the conduit of information for them both.

"No. She had a photo shoot come up so she couldn't come down after all. Do you want me to tell her to call you?" The surprise in her voice made Max curious. Maybe this was a sign things were changing if her mother had asked after her.

"No, it's fine," Aunt Dot said, and the initial inquiry in her tone had changed to resigned acceptance. "A shame she and Murphy are so busy they can't even take the time to celebrate your birthday with you! Again!"

"Aunt Dot, everything's fine. I can handle being by myself."

Aunt Dot snorted. "And you do *that* too well too."

Ira settled the phone on her chest and dropped her head back. "Aunt Dot, please."

"Yes, well, you're not getting younger, is all I'm saying. None of the children I've raised is married with families yet. I raised fine children, didn't I?"

"Yes, Aunt Dot."

"I want grandbabies!" Aunt Dot implored. "And, yes, yours and Murphy's children will count as my grandbabies!"

Max watched Ira look down at her phone and cringe. "None of us is in a place for children."

"*You* are," Aunt Dot countered. "You're the one with a steady paycheck and roots. You aren't off taking pictures or banging on some piano or getting shot at. You're smart, attractive—no good reason you aren't on baby number two with a modest ring on your finger by an upstanding man."

Max frowned, watching Ira curl into herself and she sighed harshly. "And yet here we all are."

Aunt Dot huffed. "Oh, don't be like that, Ira. I say this because I love you and I want what's best for you."

"And you think that's all tied up in a man?"

Max looked down at the spot on the floor he'd been mopping for the past three minutes, far too invested in what should probably be a private conversation now that the topic had shifted from birthday greetings to a "family meeting." But Ira didn't take the phone off speaker, and he couldn't get his feet to take him out of earshot. She sounded weary of the subject, yet her dedication to manners forced her to stay on the line instead of end the call with a flourish like Gideon no doubt would've done.

"No," Aunt Dot said finally. "That's all on you. You just have to believe you deserve it as much as I do. Actually, *more*. And while I'm sophisticated enough to acknowledge a woman's happiness isn't determined by a man, I know you want a family, eventually, Ira. Men like your uncle Elias or your dad don't grow on trees—as if they *ever* did—but you're not going to find one holed up in your apartment or in that pottery studio."

"Don't be too sure about that. Online dating is a thing now."

There was a pregnant pause. "Gideon's gotten to you, hasn't she?"

Ira laughed, and Max smiled at her gumption. "I don't mean to come across as ornery, but it *is* a thing, and it *is* possible to find love without leaving your home nowadays—or at least the beginnings of it."

"Well, let's give live interaction a try first before we fall to the mercy of AOL."

Ira laughed again. "You're dating yourself, Auntie."

"Child, I am *fine wine*. Take a sip," Aunt Dot sassed. This time, Ira's laugh was as genuine as he'd ever heard it. "There, that's what I want to hear on your birthday. It's one of my favorite days of the year, sweetheart."

Max himself was touched by the comment, rendered wistful. He'd never heard anyone say anything like that about him. In fact, he suspected his own conception and eventual birth had been a source of dread for his mother. He gripped the mop's handle tight as his thoughts spiraled down that depressing hole until pain pinched his palms and soft hands grasped his shoulders.

"Max."

He loosened the hold on the mop handle, which was now cracked, and looked up at her. Ira blinked at the destroyed handle before looking at him with concern.

"What's wrong?"

He shook his head. Delving into that would open floodgates he'd rather keep shut. He also had a personal policy while on Dream Dates: share only the bare minimum required for a connection. And since Ira had already had his dick in her mouth, there was no need to deepen it, right? However, Dream Dates also didn't happen in his private spaces, usually reserved for hotel rooms or the clients' abodes. He'd already broken a damn cardinal rule because he'd assumed he could keep his attraction to Ira on the level. Yet, it was deeper than ever now, between their intimate interlude in his kitchen earlier and being privy to such a personal conversation.

Nevertheless, he didn't want to get into his own issues. They were too fraught, too painful. He didn't want to ruin a day that had become his favorite too in such a short time. They'd keep it light; he wouldn't let it descend into darkness.

He felt cold when she pulled her hands away and held them up in surrender. "You're right; none of my business. I'm just a charity client, after all."

He glowered at her. "Ira—"

"That's not me trying to get you to say anything," she assured him with a smile that in no way reached her eyes.

"That's me reminding myself what this actually is. This is an experience, not a relationship. A *dream*." She sighed and looked down at her ruined shirt. He felt himself blush at how thoroughly he'd stained it.

"I can't believe I talked to my aunt looking like this."

"On speaker."

Ira cringed again. "I'm sorry. I feel so comfortable here that I let myself slip into familiar habits."

He brushed her apology away with a wave and a shrug. "Mi casa es tu casa. Besides, it's not like she could see you," Max said unhelpfully. He deserved her answering glare. "Washer and dryer are right in front of the landing upstairs," he tried instead. "You can drop it in if you want and I'll wash it for you."

Ira nodded, grabbing his own tank from where it was on the counter. She waved it in silent question, and he nodded.

"Thanks."

"No problem," she replied, clearing her throat. "I'mma, uh, take a shower. I should probably get dressed so I can explore the city."

Max was all for keeping her inside, in his bed, while he explored every inch of her. This wasn't his Date, though. Yet had her aunt not called, he probably would've been doing that very thing right this moment.

He'd waited too long to say something because Ira was leaving the kitchen and walking up the stairs before he registered the wide gap of silence between them. He cursed to himself as he finished straightening up the kitchen, and then he went into his bedroom to take his own shower and change. He'd just finished dressing in dark jeans and a white collared shirt when he heard the door buzz. Max went downstairs and answered the intercom.

"Package."

He rode the elevator down to the lobby, glad for the excuse to leave his condo briefly. He wasn't expecting anything; and when he saw Ira's name and Gideon's return-to address in the corner, he nodded in understanding. The box was relatively large but light; must be clothing of some sort. When he returned to the condo, he approached the guest room and debated whether to knock or leave the package at the door.

He wasn't a coward. He knocked.

Ira answered the door looking lovely and summery in a deep pink dress that set off her umber skin beautifully. She seemed to glow, and she still smelled like pineapples.

"Max?"

He shook himself to awareness and held out the package. "For you. From Gideon."

Surprised, she smiled shyly and took the box from him. "Thank you."

He remained hovering in the door while she set the package in the chair and fiddled with her phone, probably to text Gideon. He should go, but he couldn't. Their last conversation niggled at him, and he needed to clear the air between them.

"Is there something else?" Ira asked, looking back up at him again. The question was calm, incredibly polite, and made Max wince.

"This is a relationship." That had *not* been what he'd intended to say, but perhaps it was what he'd wanted to say all along.

Ira frowned at him. "What do you mean?"

"Dream Dates are an experience, yes, but they're also a relationship. Difference is, you know how long it lasts. No surprises."

She gave a half grin. "This entire experience has been one surprise after another."

He had to smile at that as well, but he entered her bedroom and stopped just before breaching her personal space. Ira averted her gaze back to her phone. Max didn't press for eye contact although he wanted it immensely. If her heart hammered with the speed and force his currently did, then he completely understood her need to gather herself. However, he wouldn't continue without her eyes on his. He needed her to see just how much he meant what he had to say.

Ultimately, Ira found enough bravery to look at him again, and he smiled. Max still didn't come closer, but he pitched his voice so the tones of it would caress her in the deepest of places.

"The whole point of Dream Dudes is so people can have the relationship they've always wanted but could never have for one reason or another. You could choose your perfect companion and have him be whoever you need him to be. Your dream literally comes true. Just because it happens instantly and lasts for a short period of time doesn't make it any less real."

Ira nodded, as if agreeing with that point, but her next words had him reeling. "I didn't choose you."

He stepped back, his heart clenching, but he recalibrated quickly. "Didn't you?"

Her scowl seemed more directed at herself than at him. "That came out wrong. I'm sorry. I meant, I chose you to help me choose a Dream Dude."

"Is that . . . not what's happening?"

She smirked at him now. "Don't we think highly of ourselves?"

He simply looked at her, his turn to smirk when she averted her gaze again and tried to hide her growing smile.

"I'm trying to keep things in perspective," she said after a moment.

"What perspective?"

She licked her lips and exhaled a deep sigh, shrugging her shoulders as she turned her eyes to the windows.

Miami was bright and almost as summery as Ira appeared, with blue skies and fluffy clouds amid other high-rise buildings. Despite the beauty, Max didn't consider it nearly as fascinating as Ira made it out to be.

"Last night, I'd told myself I could do this, go with the flow; stay in the moment. But this flow is a riptide, and it's sending me into deep waters. I ain't that strong of a swimmer, Max."

"Then stop fighting the current. You're wearing yourself out."

She scoffed. "That's easy for you to say." She crossed her arms at her chest, like she was trying to hold herself together. "You can fall in and out of love like it's nothing, but I can't do that. This ain't a job for me, Max. These are real feelings that I'm experiencing, and it's silly to indulge them when this won't last."

"Nothing lasts," he said flatly, his voice turning cold. "Everything ends; everything dies. And shame on you for thinking what I feel isn't real. The relationships may be brief, but that doesn't mean what happens during them is any less real or genuine."

She stepped back, her face falling as she gestured imploringly. "Max—"

He shook his head, holding up a hand to still her words. "And stop acting like you're the only one in this, like you're the only one who's dreading Monday. Stop acting like you're still alone behind that computer screen when

I'm here, right now, *with* you. Be here now instead of a week away. These few days are more than many folks ever get in life. I'm here and willin' to give you what you're too afraid to grasp for yourself."

"Uh, did you *miss* what happened earlier in the kitchen?"

"No," he said, coming closer, now broaching her personal space, but he still didn't touch her. "But tell me the truth: had your aunt not called, would you have let me touch you? Taste you? Would you have let me give you the pleasure you seem so fucking afraid to have for yourself?"

Eleven

This time there was no phone call to save Ira from answering or stepping up to Max's challenge. His green eyes snapped with righteous fury, and her heart felt as if it would pound out of her chest. She opened her mouth to answer, cursing the tears that stung her eyes, but she wouldn't cry in front of him. She wasn't sad so much as confused, a powerful cocktail of emotions stirred because of a simple question with a complex answer she couldn't completely articulate.

"No."

He nodded, his face set, and he stepped back. She immediately felt his absence even though he was still within arm's reach.

"See? That wasn't so hard to admit."

Her body shook with the force of her cowardice. She sat on the bed and buried her face in her hands. She only had a limited amount of time with this man on this Date, but she couldn't let go enough to enjoy it. She'd been doing so well—had even given him her first blowjob!—but that look in his eyes when he'd said he wanted to make love to her had shattered the fantasy she'd been building around herself the past twenty-four hours. Hell, it hadn't even been a full week, but she felt like she'd known Max for years. This was an illusion. He was selling her something and she'd thought she had enough to buy in, but the price was truly too high.

"If you want, I can book you a flight back to Charleston. No hard feelings."

Ira shook her head emphatically at that. "No. If it doesn't happen now, it'll probably never happen."

"If what doesn't happen?"

Ira couldn't say it. There was too much shame and disappointment and inadequacy in the confession.

She felt the air shift, and suddenly Max's hands were on her knees as he crouched down to her level. "Can I ask you something? You don't have to answer, but I think I need to at least ask."

Ira didn't pretend not to know what he wanted to know, but she supposed they had to air this out.

"Have you ever been intimate with someone before?"

She looked at him and gave him a mocking smile. "Oh, that's a copout. Just ask if I've ever had sex."

He pursed his lips, clearly unhappy with her callous tone, but he did. "Have you had sex before?"

"With a partner? No."

She said it defiantly, petulantly, but that couldn't quite mask the pathetic note she heard in her voice. Ira tried not to feel the way she did; many women hadn't had sex by her age and for various reasons. She'd made her choice not to give herself to anyone for less than what she required, and she'd stuck by it. However, the fact there seemed to be few people willing to meet the requirements really battered her ego.

"Please don't ask what's wrong with all the men in Charleston because the answer is nothing. They're perfectly fine. I'm just too picky." She pulled a face for echoing Gideon's accusation, the very accusation she'd always denied until right then.

"You like what you like," Max said evenly. "It's your body. If you have the right to be picky about anything you give others access to, it's that."

She smiled, but it was brittle and hurt her cheeks. "*This* body?"

"Yes," he said, not smiling in return, completely serious. "Your body. Your heart. *You.* That's precious, Ira, but I don't need to tell you that. I know you know that."

She did. Yes, there were times she felt insecure about herself, but that wasn't the core crux of her angst. It was a convenient and accessible excuse, though. Besides, she, Murphy, and Gideon looked enough alike that it was obvious they were related. If Gideon were beautiful enough to model, Ira knew her face wasn't going to make milk curdle, and her fat was in "all the right places." But she also knew she wasn't exactly *spectacular*, not like Gideon and her modeling or Murphy and her musical talent. She was ordinary. Rooted.

Stuck.

The frustration of being average with premium expectations; that was Ira's cross to bear.

"You also can't tell me there hasn't been interest in you," Max said softly. "I won't believe you if you did."

She smiled more genuinely this time and nodded. "There has been, and some of them were incredibly attractive—though not many. I self-sabotage a lot, probably."

"Why?"

She started to shrug, then she shook her head, deciding for complete honesty. Ira had absolutely nothing to lose by telling him this, considering their association would end in a few days. "I think they're out of my league—no, I *know* they are. They're good-looking, accomplished, everything I say I want on paper, but it's so easy to direct them elsewhere. I'm not anything dynamic or special, and I'm not saying that as someone who has low self-esteem, at least I don't think. I just . . . know what my lane is."

"What's your lane?"

"Fives to Sevens," she answered. "Maybe an Eight if I'm really feeling myself."

"Ah," he said. He stood so he could sit next to her on the bed. She didn't look at him, clasping her hands in her lap and exhaling slowly.

"What number am I? A Six? I'm at least a Six, right?"

She looked at him incredulously. "You can't be serious."

"A *Five*?"

"Max!" she cried, laughing. "You have a mirror; you know you're at least twice that!"

He shrugged. "I'm just trying to get the lay of the land, here. If I'm at least a Ten, as you say, and you think you're not, then why did The Kitchen happen?"

Ira didn't answer right away, letting herself absorb the question. "Because you touched me like I was a Ten, too, and I liked it," she admitted. "And I didn't talk myself out of enjoying the feeling. I could try something I'd always wanted to try with someone who wouldn't judge me for my lack of skill at my 'advanced' age."

He frowned, though not necessarily at her, it seemed. "I have another question, if that's okay."

She nodded. "Yeah, it's fine."

"When was the last time someone held you intimately who wasn't family, or you held them?"

"What do you mean? Like a hug?"

"A hug or something else with a potential romantic partner," he clarified. "That lasted for longer than three seconds."

She scowled at him. "Why are you getting so specific?"

"Because you're clever, and I know you're looking for loopholes."

"Three seconds ain't short for a hug."

He just eyed her and placed his hands in his lap, mimicking her. She looked away from him, a boulder suddenly finding its way into her throat, but she cleared it out the way and answered.

"Never."

"Really?"

She shook her head.

"What about holding hands?"

She shook her head again, laughing. "Never had that pleasure either." At this point, relief outweighed her embarrassment. She hadn't even told Murphy or Gideon these things, and it was liberating to share this with someone who essentially had a blank slate about her. Max had no institutional memory of her, no long list of shared experiences, and she trusted he wouldn't divulge what he'd learned. Perhaps she shouldn't have let this turn into a confessional, but maybe this was what she'd *actually* wanted for her birthday—this unburdening.

"You never met anyone you wanted to hold?" he asked.

"No, I have, but it was never mutual," she replied, "or I couldn't get over my disbelief to let it happen. It's been like trying to snap a Lego into place but it never fully clicking."

He peered at her for a moment. "I didn't mean to shrink you just now, but sometimes it's necessary. You're not the first inexperienced woman to use Dream Dudes."

"I believe that." She did. She'd done Internet searches to see how other women dealt with this, what she learned was a form of involuntary celibacy. She'd been taught to wait for the right person and the right time, but those things had never aligned. There had been times, *strong* times, when she'd wanted to hook up and get it over with, but she wasn't built for that. She greatly envied those who were, but she needed a connection and a security that what they would share would mean something more than a moment. The irony that she suspected this man who ran an escort service would be someone who put the same weight on the act as she did was inescapable.

"And you won't be the last," he continued, and she wondered if he'd said that to make her feel better. It didn't.

"But you ask these questions so you can guide them to a Dude who can handle it?"

"Yes," he said frankly. "Some Dudes are not comfortable with being Firsts. Nor do I want to pair them with those who get a thrill out of it either. The 'why' that they waited so long matters. There isn't always a sob story. Sometimes, it's just not been a priority until it becomes one. And we all know free dating sucks."

She snorted at that. "Which is why I don't do it anymore."

"I don't blame you," he said honestly, "I haven't been with anyone in over a year."

She blinked at him. "*You*. Really?"

"Yes," he affirmed. "I became bored and busy. I found I didn't really miss it."

"But you know you can attract someone," she said after a moment. "There's no danger with a hiatus for you because you know you can pull anyone you like."

"Because I'm a Ten."

"Yes."

His smile was wry. "I've been trying to reel you in for the past day and you keep fighting me."

"I'm a job, though."

His laugh was humorless. "You weren't kidding about the self-sabotage, were you?"

Ira winced. "I'm sorry."

"Why don't you trust you can also reel in whoever you want?"

She shrugged, her earlier relief starting to become weariness. "What would I offer a partner, Max? I'm not beautiful like Gideon, although I've been told repeatedly I'm 'cute'; I'm not remotely talented like my sister, although my pottery is unique because not a lot of people do it. I'm not 'enhancing' anyone's life, building up their social cache. I'm just *there*. I'd just *be there*."

"And you don't think that matters?"

"I think why settle when you can get the best?"

He nodded once. "And you feel a little like a hypocrite because you demand the best for yourself but don't think you'd be the best for someone else."

"Whew," she said, laughing to hide just how on the mark he was. "You should've been a psychologist."

He grinned. "That was my major in college."

"You're g-d Twelve is what you are. Get outta my face."

He laughed and she smiled. "I wasn't always a Twelve."

"I don't believe you."

"I'm so serious," he said. "I didn't become the Twelve you think me to be until I had people affirm who I always thought I could be. Strangers. Although I don't understand why we dismiss what our loved ones tell us unless it's negative, I do understand needing that affirmation from outside people. I think we interpret it as more genuine, that they're not saying it just because they love us and want us to be happy; they're saying it because it's true for them."

"And if it's true for them, it must be the reality of things," Ira finished. "That's it *exactly*. I thought once I hit my thirties, I'd stop caring what other people thought of me. That's what Aunt Dot said would happen, anyway."

"But it hasn't."

"No," she said with a sigh. "It hasn't."

"Why do you think that is? Because I can admit I feel a little of the same way."

She lifted her shoulders and let them drop heavily. That was a good question, one she hadn't exactly pondered for any length of time. But maybe deconstructing it for an answer would help put a lot of things in perspective.

"I have a theory," he said. "May I share it with you?"

"By all means," she said, then she laughed a little. "Maybe birthdays bring out our philosophical natures."

He grinned as well. "I think there are people who need to find someone they're in tune with—not just ideas or thinking, but spirits. And if the spirit isn't settled, nothing else will work."

He held out his hand. "Like there's that Great Tuning Fork that was struck before we were all born, and some of us look for those persons that we harmonize the best with—that *one chord.* Yeah, there are other chords that work and even sound nice, but it's not *that chord.* Some of us settle for those other chords and that's fine; but some of us can't, for whatever reason. And then we internalize that lack of harmony and think we're the ones out of tune, and that this means we are inherently faulty or lacking, but we're not. Because then we find *that chord . . .*"

His hand was now at her thigh, palm up, and her eyes stung. Her heart thundering in her chest, Ira pressed her palm to his, their fingers interlocking.

"Sweet, sweet music, ain't it?" he whispered, bringing up their joined hands to kiss her knuckles.

Twelve

I ra rarely let go of Max's hand throughout the rest of the day, and he didn't mind this one bit. He hadn't meant to get so heavy with her, to grill her, but he'd needed answers for why she was resisting the very thing she craved. Part of him now realized she'd simply been overwhelmed. For someone with that little experience, the headiness of everything could require the use of a pause button. He'd taken it far too personally, but he'd already reached a revelation she couldn't trust herself to believe.

They were attuned to each other because they were meant for each other.

He didn't make that pronouncement out loud, realizing she was already at the limit of her ability to process what was happening, but he understood this fact to his bones. He'd been here before, and the fallout of that had taken him over a year to recover from it. At least then, that person hadn't been completely new to everything. Ira was a far more delicate case and he had to proceed with caution.

"*Ooh*, this is pretty."

The flower she was admiring was almost the same color as her dress, called a *Pachypodium baronii* according to its placard. There were five petals that looked like they'd been crumpled up and stretched out again. If she wanted to call it pretty, that was fine with him. Aside from its striking color, Max didn't see anything truly distinctive about it.

They were at the Fairchild Tropical Botanic Gardens about thirty minutes south of Miami. Ira had suggested the outing, wanting something to do that wasn't typical "Miami" as she'd never been much of a clubber, and she admired nature.

"I work with dirt, after all," she'd said on the drive down. "Me and Mother Earth are tight."

"But you don't like bugs."

"We all have our inconsistencies, Max."

He let her guide him around the gardens, and he watched her more than the colorful and verdant plants surrounding them. She came alive looking at the pretty flora, her smile wide and her hand squeezing his as they stopped at one plant or another. Max stayed close, not letting her stray far enough that he couldn't touch her. He wanted her used to his touch, to the physical manifestation of his regard for her that wasn't wrapped up in lust.

He was glad they'd cleared much of the air earlier and was humbled Ira had trusted him enough to tell him those things. He realized now she had been trying to overcompensate for much and he'd been letting her, desperate for her in a way he hadn't been for someone in a long time. But then, as she'd said, she'd gotten in too deeply and her flailing had caught him off guard. He shouldn't have been as upset as he'd been. Plenty of clients had backed out of Dates before when things had gotten too hot to handle. That he'd taken Ira's rejection personally was yet another sign Ira wasn't remotely a job or a favor or anything else so clinical.

She was his harmony.

Max stepped behind her and pressed his lips to the back of her head, closing his eyes at the contact. Ira leaned back into him and sighed. They were standing on a bridge overlooking a waterscape that was filled with waterlilies and other colorful plants. They'd been at the gardens for about two hours and honestly, he was over the trip now. Not to say what he'd seen hadn't been lovely, but he was anxious to get Ira alone again. He wanted her, obviously, but he more wanted to pamper her until maybe—just maybe—she'd forget all about her train ride back to Charleston Monday morning.

"Ready to go?" he asked against her short-cropped hair. It was soft against his lips and smelled very nice, sweet but not too cloying.

She chuckled, palming his hip with a squeeze. "Are you all natured out?"

"Yeah," he confessed, dipping his mouth to her ear. "I want to be alone with you."

Ira turned her head to look at him, a small smile on her face. "So you can do what?"

He grinned and brushed his nose against hers. "Pamper you."

Her eyes brightened at that. "*Ooh*, like a massage?"

He nodded. "Would you like that?"

"Yep," she said, grinning. "I haven't had one in such a long time. Do you give good ones?"

He held up a hand and shrugged. "Not had many complaints about them. I'm actually certified."

Ira held his hand in both of hers, letting her index finger trace along the lines of his palm. "This is a strong hand. I like holding it."

"It likes you holding it too."

She smiled and kissed the center of his palm. "We can go. We've been out here for hours and I'm afraid your sunscreen is going to wear off soon."

He smiled, remembering how thorough she'd been with her application of it. She'd made sure she'd gotten every nook and cranny of his face, ears, neck, and arms.

He did his own legs and feet, not wanting her to kneel before him again. His cock had started twitching under her care and he hadn't wanted them getting derailed.

"Before we go, though," he said, pulling out his phone. "We need a selfie."

"Selfie won't get all the pretty!" Ira insisted and managed to recruit a fellow visitor to take the picture that would capture them and the nature behind them. The young teen snapped three photos and Ira thanked her while he retrieved the phone.

"You're super hot," the young girl gushed. "There's hope for me yet!"

Max just smiled, not wanting to ask what she meant but having a good idea anyway. He frowned at the device he held as he went back to Ira.

"Are they bad?" she asked, slight panic in her voice. "Your face says they're bad."

He blinked and shook his head. "I don't think so."

Max pulled up the photos. They were basically the same shot of him with his cheek pressed against Ira's and his arms around her waist. Ira looked gorgeous for her part, a bright smile to go with bright eyes. He smiled as well, but it was much more contented than Ira's eager one. He looked at peace and pleased.

"We look good," Ira declared. "Send it to me? I'm not even gonna send it to Gideon. This is just for *me*."

"I still want my selfie," he said, putting the settings on his phone so the picture would snap on a timer. He held it out so the camera would capture them both, but he turned his head just before the shutter clicked to kiss the space by her nose. The resulting photograph was of a grinning Max smooshing his face into Ira's scrunched-up one.

"We look absolutely ridiculous," Ira critiqued, laughing as they made their way out the gardens. "I'm *definitely* not sending that one to Gideon!"

"It's my favorite," Max determined. "Might make that my lock screen."

She looked at him, surprise stark on her face. "Are you serious?"

He didn't look at her as he changed the settings on his phone so that his lock screen now showed their awkward, laughing faces. He presented his phone to her and earned her arm weaving around his and her lips against his shoulder.

Ira dozed on the drive back to his condo, but her hand remained linked with his. He ran his thumb across her knuckles, the ability to touch her comforting. The sun streamed into the car, hitting her dark skin in such a way that she seemed to glow. The gentle swells of her breasts pressed against the bodice of her dress, and the dress's straps curved around bared, generous shoulders.

He'd wanted his mouth on those shoulders, those swells, all damn day, but he maintained a safe distance.

Ira shifted, squeezing her fingers around his, but didn't awaken. He'd had plans for them, having called ahead to one of his favorite restaurants to reserve a table. But he didn't want to go there anymore. He didn't want to share her, but she deserved a nice dinner for her birthday. Leftovers weren't going to cut it.

They were a block away from his condo when Max roused Ira from her light nap. She stretched and smiled, cradling his hand in her lap.

"This car is a problem," she said, her voice raspy. "Every time I get in here, I fall asleep."

"You make for a boring driving partner," he said with mock seriousness, and he laughed when she sucked her teeth and let go of his hand.

"Nope," he chastised, grasping her hand again. "Least I can do is hold you while you sleep. You owe me *some* form of connection."

She chuckled and placed their joined hands upon her belly, looking out of her passenger window. "Least you can do, huh?"

Minutes later they were back in his condo, both of them in the kitchen as they drank glasses of water. He let her check his face to make sure his face hadn't started blistering, and he basked in her care. He felt fine; the SPF 75 she'd applied had been more than enough to protect his skin. Yet Ira was a nurturer, greedy to care for someone. He submitted wholeheartedly.

"I see why you're a nurse," he murmured when she pulled away. "You're a worrywart."

"Am not," she said, laughing. "Just that sunburn's not fun."

"Have close and intimate experience with that, do you?"

"You know how many folk with peeling, blistering skin come into urgent care? Yes, sir, I do!"

They laughed and Max shook his head. "You can admit you're a worrywart. Gids has told me stories."

Her face fell slightly, and Max squeezed her hand. She shrugged. "Maybe connecting us is her way to make a return on investment."

Max shook his head. "This isn't payback, Ira."

She nodded and looked at their interlocked fingers. "Aunt Dot still doesn't know I gave Gideon money. Or Murphy. She just thinks they ran off half-cocked, chasin' pipe dreams. But sometimes you gotta chase until you can reach them, right? It wasn't even a lot of money, just enough to help out with their rents for a few months until they got steady gigs."

"That's plenty," Max said quietly. "That's more than a lot of people get to go pursue a dream."

She nodded, then shook her head. "I should tell Aunt Dot I gave them money."

"Why?"

"You heard that earlier phone call," she said. "Today is one of her favorite days. Would she still feel that way if she learned I aided and abetted her girls into careers she doesn't like?"

"Those lives ain't hers to live," Max said. "Do you know how precious it is to have someone who believes in you? Ira, you gave them both so much more than money, far more valuable."

Ira nodded and smiled, this one more genuine. "I'm so proud of them."

Max kissed her temple. "Now, enough about them. This is still your day, easin' into night. What else would you like?"

Ira shrugged and smiled cheekily. "What else do you have planned?"

He gave her a mild glare at her teasing, but then softened his expression when she nuzzled his cheek. "I have reservations for us at a restaurant on the water, if you want to go out."

"I'm not really hungry," she admitted. "I mean, not enough to shower and change and go out, because I'm sure it's fancy."

He arched an eyebrow. "It could be a McDonald's on the water for all you know."

"Bye, Max."

He laughed and conceded her point. "Fine. Would you like for me to order in again?"

"Isn't that awful?" she asked with a nod. "In Miami and all I wanna do is stay in and eat takeout. I could've done that in Moncks Corner."

"But *I'm* not in Moncks Corner."

"You could've gotten on a train just like I did, sir. Try again."

Chuckling, Max stood directly in front of her and wrapped an arm around her waist. "I would've flown."

"Oooh, look at you with your disposable income to take pop-up trips," she teased more. Her lips were pliant for his kiss. "You don't mind if we stay in, though, do you?"

"Nope," he said against her mouth. "Why do you think I rushed you home?"

She pulled back, her smile shy. "You want to give me a massage that bad?"

He kissed her again, this time doing his best to caress every crevice of her mouth with his tongue. When he broke it, she swayed and sighed, burying her nose in the crook of his neck and shoulder.

"I wanna make you feel good that bad."

She brought her smiling mouth to his ear. "Your bedroom or mine?"

Thirteen

M ax's bedroom wasn't that much larger than the guest bedroom, but it felt like him. The décor was silver and black with blackout shades and drapes covering every window wall available—which was three of the room's four sides. It helped set the mood, as did the candles flickering all about, casting gold and amber hues about the space. Ambient sounds played as well.

"This isn't a fire hazard?"

Max chuckled. "They're electric, although there is incense burning. Jasmine. That's real."

He stood shirtless behind her, and she could feel his warm skin on the bared sections of her back exposed by the black floral chemise she wore. It'd been Gideon's birthday gift to her, and part of Ira wondered if this were always going to be her gift or the one Gideon gotten in the hopes something would happen between her and Max once she'd learned how Ira would be spending her birthday weekend. Truthfully, the chemise wasn't really that sexy, but it was far more feminine than the T-shirt and yoga pants that were her usual sleep attire. Bonus point that Max did like it, his eyes having traveled over her form as if he couldn't wait to tear it off.

She linked her fingers with his as they stood at his bed. The covers were pulled down and a black bath sheet was laid out in the center of the bed. There were oils and lotions on the nightstand that she didn't recognize, and her body trembled with nerves and anticipation.

"You don't have to take off your nightgown," he said.

"Would it be better if I did?"

"Yes, but we'll work with your comfort level."

She looked over her shoulder into his green eyes. Though she could see the lust, she mostly saw a man who wanted to give her the best massage possible. She just had to be open enough to receive it.

Ira nodded. "Okay. Can you give me a second?"

Max didn't smile or smirk, just nodded and kissed her forehead. "Holler when you're ready. You can keep your panties on, and we'll decide if you want a full-body one once we get started."

Ira's heart thudded in her chest as she drew down the chemise's bodice and lay upon the towel, her nipples brushing against the soft terry cloth. She couldn't relax, her body bow-tight, but she curled her arms around the pillow underneath her cheek and took a large breath before calling in Max.

She drew on her bravery and faced him as he entered. It felt slightly uncomfortable to lie on her belly and breasts, but she knew it would be worth it. He crouched down so they were eye level, and his large, warm palm found the center of her back.

"Hi," he whispered. "You're really soft."

She laughed, hiding half of her face further into the pillow. "You have good soap."

Chuckling, he kissed her nose when she revealed her face again, then drifted down to meet her lips with his. "You're tense too. Relax. This'll be good; I promise."

Max knew exactly what to do with his hands. Every kink and knot in her body he found and massaged right out, using the precise amount of pressure to accomplish the job. He combined firm kneads with comforting strokes, making her body feel like jelly. She became so slack she drooled, and she'd discretely wipe her mouth and cheeks against her arm. Nothing was under her power anymore. Max possessed her completely.

Ira didn't shift or shudder when he moved down to her legs. His powerful hands running over her thick limbs made her sigh and snuggle into her pillow. She did jerk slightly when he found her foot, and she grinned as he kissed the instep.

"I forgot you're ticklish," he said in a low voice.

"Forgiven, as long as you keep them hands on me."

He gave the backs of her legs a firm glide upward, and Ira let out the most decadent moan. Max didn't stop until the backs of his hands were wedged into the curve of her ass underneath her chemise's skirt.

He stopped.

"Ira?"

"Yes?"

His fingers caressed the curve of her behind, and she clenched her derriere's muscles in response. She whined softly when he removed his hands from her but didn't have the energy to glare at him like she wanted. She felt too replete with relaxation to do so.

"What's wrong?" she asked when he still hadn't continued the massage.

"Would you like the full-body massage?"

The words were whispered, barely heard over the gurgling brook sounds coming from his Bose sound dock. Ira shivered. The space between her legs, which had been growing slicker by the moment, was suddenly as streaming as that brook.

"What does that entail?" The question was more breath than voice.

"I massage you everywhere."

His voice was deep and raspy, and she wanted to curl into it. Ira took a deep breath and held the pillow tighter.

"And everywhere means *everywhere*? With just your hands."

"Not the massage I want to give."

She shuddered and whimpered, especially when his hot breath found the center of her back before his lips did. Her fingers and toes went tense, and she let out a choked breath. Those kisses continued up her spine until they curved over her shoulder and his full lips brushed against the shell of her ear.

"I wanna stroke you everywhere. With *everything*."

Her brain froze, needing the pause to untangle exactly what he was telling her. She then frowned when a potential revelation hit, and she hugged the pillow underneath her ear.

"Are you askin' to have sex with me?"

He grimaced and cupped the back of her head. She wondered why she felt so safe with his hold like that. "Baldly put but yes. If you allow me to give you the massage I really want, sex is highly likely."

"Will you stop if I change my mind?"

Max's face darkened, but his hand remained tender, as did his voice when he replied. "I hate you even have to ask that, but I understand. I hate there are people out there who don't honor another person's words or decisions. I always will, Ira. And yes, if you change your mind, I'll stop immediately. I'd never force you, especially not with this. You've held out this long for a reason and I respect it."

Ira smiled, her heart expanding in her chest. "I distinctly remember tellin' you there was never a mutual regard for it."

"Well, if I may be so bold, I think there's one now, right?"

Still smiling, Ira gathered her courage and turned her head to kiss him. His lips were soft and yielding beneath hers even as the hold on her head grew stronger. She felt incredibly safe with him. She trusted him with her body and a large portion of her heart too.

"Turn over," he whispered against her lips.

Ira didn't hesitate, feeling a thrill rush through her body as her front became exposed to the temperate air of his bedroom. Max kept his eyes to hers and his hand moved from the back of her head to her cheek.

"You're so lovely," he whispered, frowning a little. "What is it about you, Ira Jackson?"

She shook her head, reaching out to drift her fingers along his lush mouth and strong cheeks. "What is it about *you*?"

Eyes still locked with hers, Max kissed her fingers as his oiled hands found her body once more. They were warm and slick on her torso, and she stretched in response. Max grinned at her, his hands moving from her sides to her hips and back again. Ira purred like a cat so resplendent she felt.

"So far, so good?" he asked teasingly.

"If you've done this with your other clients, my reaction shouldn't be a surprise," she tossed back breathlessly.

"I'm not worried about their reactions right now," he said against her nose. "Only yours."

Ira sighed and accepted his kiss, letting her legs spread as he continued to knead down her leg. Her pussy throbbed, wanting his hands there instead of on her fleshy thighs and her fairly muscular calves.

His touch was different now, striving to arouse instead of relax. He squeezed her with purpose, making her shiver and gasp, yet he didn't stray from the safe areas of her body. His green eyes remained on her face, as if content with the feel of her without needing to look. Ira wanted to hide from his gaze as much as she wanted to bask in it.

She hadn't realized she'd closed her eyes until he removed his hands and they popped open. Ira frowned at him for two seconds before she realized he was undressing. He was so beautiful, built like a statue of apex masculinity. She curled her hands into the pillow beneath her head, unsure of the rules for her. Could she touch him like he touched her? Was she just a recipient in this interlude or could she give too?

"Jesus," she whispered, her eyes widening as she realized he was getting completely naked. His thick erection bobbed against his lower belly, the head of it pointing to his navel. Her mouth watered, wanting the turgid flesh between her lips again. He really had the most beautiful cock she'd ever seen.

"I thought I was the one giving the massage."

Max's voice was sandpaper rough and the comment confused her, but then Ira saw she had her hand between her legs—fingers in the proverbial cookie jar. She blushed hard, glad her skin was dark enough to hide it, but she didn't yank them out of her panties. In fact, she spread her legs wider and moved the crotch of them aside so he could get a better look at her most intimate place. Could he see how wet and gooey she was? Could he tell the difference between his oil and her arousal? Did he notice how large her clit was, swollen with need for his fingers? His lips? His cock?

"Keep goin'," he commanded, his voice still gruff even as his Southern drawl became more pronounced. His eyes were riveted upon the space between her legs, and Ira didn't realize she could experience such a freeing thrill at being watched. She circled her plump middle finger once around her engorged nubbin before dipping into her wetness and bringing the coated finger back to it again. The friction eased, allowing the finger to glide around the sensitive flesh, and her mouth fell open at the unfettered desire Max had on his face from watching her.

"You like gentle touches," he rumbled. "Occasional firm pressure, but you like to be teased. You like it to sneak up on you."

"Yes," she confirmed in a whisper, matching his quiet tone. Birdsong from the sound system filled the space now.

He came to the side of the bed and kneeled, his chin hovering above her hip. He kissed the top of her thigh as he gripped it and pulled it toward her. She was even more exposed now, but she didn't stop her fingers. She felt herself throb and leak onto the towel.

"You're so fuckin' responsive," he said on a choked whisper, his kiss gentle upon the inside of her slick thigh. "You're so beautiful, Ira. Fuck."

Her fingers moved faster the higher up her thigh he kissed until his mouth found the crease between her leg and hip. He nuzzled her there, and her body began to shake. Her climax was in reach, hovering for her to grasp, but she was afraid to grab it. This much pleasure frightened her, admittedly; and with Max here with her, it was sure to overwhelm.

Ira squeezed her eyes shut, her fingers slowing, the climax that had been hurtling toward her banking left. She exhaled a harsh breath, though she wasn't sure if it were in relief or frustration. Something must be truly wrong with her if she couldn't even climax with a handsome partner helping her along!

"What's wrong?" he asked against her hip.

Ira shook her head. "I can't."

The mattress shifted under Max's weight as he climbed completely into bed with her. He was hot against her, yet comforting, and she curled her body into his. He cuddled her with one arm and let his free hand glide up and down her side.

"You can't what?" he asked against her temple.

She hid her face into his neck. "Come. I can't. I'm scared."

"Of what?"

"Of feeling too much. I feel like I'mma pass out."

"You might," he said plainly. "If it's a really good one."

Ira sucked her teeth but grinned against his skin at his chuckle.

"Have you ever climaxed before?"

She shook her head. "I always stop before I do."

"Darlin', that's just no way to live."

She had to laugh at his tortured tone. "Shut up!"

He laughed as well, then sat up and asked her to do the same. She did and let him move her until he was directly behind her. He cradled her in his hold. His erection speared her lower back, and he grasped her wrist before she could touch him.

"This is about you right now," he insisted against her cheek. "I want you to do something for me. Or rather, let me do something for you."

"What?"

"Let me give you an orgasm."

Fourteen

Max literally felt Ira balk at the request. Her spine stiffened, and she faced him with a quelling glare. He looked at her placidly, holding out a placating hand.

"Can I explain what I mean?"

Her glare was unrelenting. "Please.

"Not that I mean to set the women's lib movement back a few decades, but I think your issue is you need to cede control and you've not felt safe enough to do it. Or maybe you haven't given permission to do it. If you give that control to me, you'd be forced to take what I give you."

"You mean like BDSM?"

He arched an eyebrow. "Not something as formal as that. I haven't been trained, but you can let me push you to what you can stand and see if we can't push those limits so you can experience everything. If you want a safe word, we can do that. Just know I'm gonna challenge you on it if I think you're wussing out."

Ira looked away and drew her knees to her chest. Max couldn't help stroking her back with his palm. Her skin really was soft, made even more so from the oil he'd massaged into her. He loved having his hands and mouth on her. She felt and tasted delicious.

"Can 'happy birthday' be the safe word?"

"That's a mouthful," he said against her shoulder.

"I know," Ira said, turning her head so their noses met. "I'd have to really mean it if I say it."

"I won't think less of you if you do," he said. "This is a lot. And I'll confess—I passed out when I had my first orgasm."

Her eyes widened, and she pulled her lips into her mouth to hide her smile. Max rolled his eyes at her amusement, but he continued the story.

"At the tender age of thirteen, I was in the shower, and I started my . . . *exploration* . . . and perhaps that wasn't the best place to do it."

"You slipped?"

"Dropped like a sack of potatoes and hit my head. To this day that's been the most embarrassing hospital visit I've ever had in my life."

Explaining to his seventy-year-old foster mother what he'd been doing to knock himself out bare-ass naked in the shower hadn't been one of his finer moments, but Selena Worthington had given him The Talk without too much laughter at his expense yet with a treasure trove of understanding.

"Mama Worthington had even told me I should just stick to a chair or a bed from now on," Max recalled with a slight chuckle. "I did, and at least I'd improved my coordination and my stamina."

"Mama Worthington?" Ira asked. "Is that how you distinguished your paternal and maternal grandparents?"

Max's smile faded and he shook his head. "I didn't know my grandparents."

Confusion crossed her face before some sort of understanding overcame her visage. Sympathy full in her eyes, Ira kissed his forehead. "We don't have to talk about it."

"Good call," he said, not wanting to confirm whatever conclusion she'd drawn right then. "Besides, the conversation's a real mood killer and I wanna give you several orgasms for your birthday."

Ira rolled her eyes but grinned. "You're so generous."

"I aim to be," he whispered right before pressing his lips to hers.

His arms wrapped around her bare waist as they continued to kiss, Ira's back pressed completely against his front as the lip lock grew more intense. Max contented himself with stroking her soft belly. He relished the feel of it, as well as the sighs and moans she made at his touch. He scooted them both back until he rested against the bed's headboard, and then he spread her legs until they were draped over his. He looked down the line of her body, over her abundant sloping hills, until he spied the glistening skin of her inner thighs. He grasped her right hand—the hand that had been giving herself pleasure earlier—and sucked the digits of it in his mouth. Her fingers were salty, tangy, addicting. He groaned around them.

"Max," she gasped, grinding against him. His cock felt hard enough to break through diamonds, but he actually liked the anticipation of completion. He refused to think of her mouth around him, though. He'd lose it if he did.

He grasped her panties and did a tug to ask for permission. She nodded and lifted her hips to slip off her panties. Once they were free from her body, he resettled her so that her legs were once more draped over his, leaving her open.

"Touch yourself again," Max commanded, placing her fingers back at the core of her. "You're gonna help me give you this orgasm."

Ira released a small sigh, but her fingers began to strum the space between her legs as if it were guitar strings. She made such sweet music, yipping and moaning as her pleasure began to grow again. He sucked on her shoulder, tasting the salt and the oil on his tongue, while his hands smoothed up her belly to cup her breasts.

"Oh," she gasped, pressing her back harder into his chest.

"You like that?" he asked, squeezing the plump mounds before drifting tender fingers upon the points of her dark nipples. They looked delicious and his mouth watered for them, but he couldn't move yet—not until Ira fell over the edge.

"Max," she said on a harsh breath and her fingers moved faster.

"I love the way you feel," he said, keeping his voice low and heavy in her ear. He began to buck into the small of her back and she met his thrust with her own. "I love how responsive you are. You feel it that much, baby?"

Ira sighed again, dropping her head back onto his shoulder and exposing her neck. Grunting, Max licked up its column before sucking at the hinge of her jaw. She shuddered against him and inhaled sharply, but Max didn't think she'd come yet. He tangled his fingers with hers between her legs to confirm his suspicion. She shuddered more and was still very wet, but she wasn't sopping yet. Then again, not every woman flowed like a gushing river when she climaxed.

"Have you come yet?" he asked, unable to stop his thumb from finding her swollen clit. It felt large enough to get a good grip on with his mouth and his tongue tingled with want.

"I don't think so," she confessed. "But I'm close."

"You are? What can I do to bring you over?"

She shook her head against his shoulder. Her hips also began pulling away and her fingers slowed.

"No," he said firmly, staying her hips. "Don't run away from it. It won't hurt you."

"Max!" she choked out, squeezing her eyes shut. "I can't!"

"You can't or you don't want to?" Max asked, banding a strong arm around her middle.

"It's too much! It's too much!" Ira cried, her voice thick with her tears. "Happy birthday!"

Max loosened his arm immediately. Though she'd said the safe word, he would've released her anyway. She'd no longer sounded like a woman on the brink of ecstasy; instead, she'd sounded terrified.

Max gently removed Ira's hands from between her legs and then turned her so she cuddled into him. She adjusted herself until she lay completely atop him chest to chest, her face hidden in the crook of his neck while the shudders eased out of her body.

Night sounds drifted from the speakers, mixing with Ira's calming breaths. Max stroked a soothing hand along her back while she nosed his jaw. His erection had softened at Ira's distress and his cock rested between their thighs. He kissed her forehead tenderly and she sighed.

"I ruined it."

Max frowned at the ceiling. "Ruined what?"

"We were supposed to have sex and I ended up crying all over you."

He shrugged and continued stroking her back. "You're not the first to cry and you won't be the last. It can be overwhelming, sharing something this intimate with someone you barely know. You did nothing wrong. Maybe I demanded too much of you unfairly."

Ira shook her head. "No, you set the terms and I agreed to them. You did everything right; I'm the broken one."

"I don't think you're broken."

She scoffed then and shook her head as she rose. She ended up straddling his hips and the view of her was spectacular. He couldn't keep his hands to himself, shifting his strokes from her back to her thighs.

"You're handsome, considerate, patient, knowledgeable, and not even *that* is enough for me to let go and enjoy this? C'mon, Max, even you have to admit that's really off!"

Max shrugged and squeezed her hips. "Okay, so we're all a little broken in some ways, baby. A hairline fracture here, a complete shatter there. We all stitch ourselves together differently."

Her hands settled on his pectorals, and she frowned down at him. "I don't have a traumatic backstory, Max."

He kept his expression level. "Gideon said differently."

Ira pursed her lips and looked off to the side. After taking a deep breath, Ira shook her head. "I mean, *sexually*."

Max nodded. Many of his clients couldn't say the same. Hell, *he* couldn't say the same. He frowned at that and sat up, keeping her close, until they were chest to chest again. "Climaxes are cathartic. Or they can be."

Ira matched his frown, but he couldn't help his small smile when her fingers found the nape of his neck once more and tangled in his curls. "I'm not trying to get a free therapy session from you, Max."

"I know," he said, "and I'm not trained in that, either, but you learn a lot in this business. You figure out what makes people go, and then you end up being a therapist whether you want to be or not. I think you might need one."

"*Thanks.*"

He laughed at her derision, though not unkindly. "There's no shame in that, Ira. I have one."

She blinked at him, her strokes at his nape pausing. "Yeah?"

Nodding, he found her collarbone with his lips. "Unfortunately, I *do* have a traumatic backstory. And it *is* sexual in nature, though not only that."

Ira froze, becoming rigid in his arms, and he kissed her collarbone again. "Escorting started out as a way to work through that, with a smattering of oedipal complexes for good measure."

She hugged him tightly. "You don't have to tell me this."

"I'm not ashamed," Max said, although he trembled and held her just as tightly. "It's not my shame even though I've carried it for so long. It ain't mine, Ira, but I picked it up anyway. It was the only thing of my parents I'd had left."

She turned her face into his cheek, her hand cradling his free one, and he sighed into her hold. "Have you told any of your clients this?"

"No," he said. "I probably never will, simply because it's about *them*, not me."

"But you want to tell me?" Ira asked. "Even though this weekend is supposed to be about me?"

She wasn't being selfish with the question, and she did have a right to ask it. Sighing, Max turned his head to brush his lips against hers, Ira's fingers still gentle on his cheeks.

"When clients want to be vulnerable, I give them the space to do so. Usually, I tell them something that's vulnerable enough to get them to trust me. But it's never too deep of a heart matter because that's usually not what the connection is. I have to give in order for them to feel comfortable giving, and it has to be something that doesn't make a mockery of them."

"And it's confidential?"

"Absolutely," Max said, looking directly into her eyes. "That would damage both parties if the trust isn't absolute."

"I understand," Ira said after a moment, "but this is a deep heart matter. For you."

"Yeah."

"And you trust me with this?"

"Yes," he said, grasping her chin gently. "I've told Gideon. Well, not all of it, but enough."

"Oh," Ira said, "but you wanna tell me all of it?" At his nod, her confusion really overcame her face. "Why?"

"Because as bare as we are right now, I wanna strip myself down as far as I can go. Maybe if I do that, you'll be comfortable enough to do it with me."

"And what if a client doesn't want that? Or is too afraid anyway?"

"I don't push," he said. "I never push, but I've also never had the urge to tell them what I wanna tell you."

She shook her head, pulling back so she could meet his gaze. "I don't want you to tell me."

His heart squeezed painfully. "Why?"

"I don't want you to tap into that hurt. This is supposed to be fun and light and *relaxing*—not deep and serious!"

"If you don't let yourself feel hurt, you can't feel joy," Max said. "Whatever hurt you're tryin' to avoid, remember: it's already happened. It can't hurt you any worse than it did then."

She shook her head. "Some of it hasn't happened yet."

"But you're so scared of it," he said, confused. "What's got you so terrified? It's not the orgasm, is it? Not really."

"But like you said, it's a catharsis."

"Catharsis is good."

Ira looked down, drawing her hand from his face to place against his chest. His heart thundered underneath her palm so fiercely she must feel it.

"I'll feel too much; I know I will," she said quietly. "I already do. I feel *so* much, Max, and I should've known better."

Max's heart surged into his throat, but he managed to swallow enough of it down to get out his next words. "Known better about what?"

"About falling in love with you. I don't know if I'll ever be able to bounce back from it."

Fifteen

Ira could admit the big pit of dread that had filled her stomach shrank a little at that confession. Catharsis *was* good, but only if channeled properly. Fucking Max into oblivion without admitting this would've had the absolute opposite effect for her. Yet even with the confession, Ira didn't feel completely unburdened because Max had been right; she might not have the same type of trauma Max had experienced, but it was trauma nonetheless, one that made her incapable of feeling the complete depths and ranges of her emotions for fear of being overwhelmed.

Which then *further* terrified her because what she felt for Max was pretty damn intense.

For his part, Max remained as neutral as ever upon her declaration, which made Ira feel relief and a little dismay. He hadn't twitched, smiled, frowned, laughed—anything—that could give her a clue as to how he felt about it. He just gazed at her and caressed her body with the same soothing strokes he'd been using for the past few minutes.

"I'm not the first woman to have fallen in love with you, I'm sure," she said after a moment of heavy silence.

"No," he said softly.

His hands were so very tender on her; they made her feel dear. She closed her eyes and averted her face, squeezing his pectorals because she needed to touch him.

"Honestly, I thought this would be a weekend like all the other dates I'd had; maybe with a lil' more kissin' and touchin', but not this. If I'd thought this would've happened, I probably wouldn't've come."

"The prospect of fallin' in love with me was that bad?"

Ira began to shake her head, but then she shrugged. "I've been on a yo-yo all weekend: one minute tellin' myself I can have this fling and the next knowing I can't. I've tried to be brave and power through this, but I keep gettin' stuck."

"You power through loving someone?"

Ira glared at him now, then she sighed. "We just met, and this won't last."

"Nothing lasts," Max said to her, though not unkindly. "Everything ends. I thought we established that already."

They had, and then her mind snatched upon something else he'd said.

"Max?"

He suddenly smiled then, sliding his hands up her body to cradle the back of her head. "Yes, darlin'."

His name hadn't been the question, and his reply made her frown even as she chuckled. "What are you tellin' me yes for?"

"Fine, you're right. Ask me the question," he said, coming closer to kiss her cheek. He caressed the back of her head with one hand while his other arm squeezed her closer. She wrapped her arms around his neck and hugged him closer.

"You're dreadin' Monday too?"

"Yes."

"Because you'll miss me."

"Yes."

"Because you have feelings for me."

"Yes."

"That aren't just lust."

"Yes."

"And you've felt this before with other people."

"Yes."

"But that doesn't make that any less real or valid with me."

"Yes."

"And even after we part, these feelings are real, even if we couldn't share them together for long."

"Yes."

Ira nodded and hid her face into his neck. "Murphy and I were fightin'. We were supposed to go on a gig with our parents—they were a gospel duo that traveled all over—but because we were actin' out, Mama and Daddy took us to Aunt Dot and Uncle Elias's for punishment while they went alone. They never came back. And intellectually, I know they still loved us even though they were angry and disappointed. But they didn't say, 'I love you' when they left. And I didn't say it to them."

That had been twenty years ago, and she'd never shared this with a soul. Aunt Dot wouldn't really let the conversation come up, everyone remembering those last moments they'd all had with each other. Her cousin Jerome hadn't even come downstairs to greet his aunt and uncle, too busy playing a video game, and Gideon had been over at a friend's house. Talking to Murphy about it was out of the question, especially when she couldn't even remember what their argument had been about. All Ira could think was her parents had been so upset with them that they weren't completely paying attention to the road. That was why her father had run the red light and into the path of an oncoming tow truck.

"You were loved, Ira," Max said quietly. "And you are loved. It's not conditional; it just is."

"I know," Ira said, but tears stung her eyes. The amount of crying she'd been doing this weekend made her supremely uncomfortable, but perhaps she'd been long overdue to shed these tears. "I know they knew I loved them—me and Murphy—but we were so bad. I was too bad. It wouldn't have happened if we weren't bad."

"Or maybe they were meant to die anyway and if you and your sister would've been in that car, I wouldn't have had the chance to fall in love with you either."

Ira hugged Max tighter, letting his words sink into her heart and fill her with light. She wanted to ask if he was sure; if he were just saying the words because she wanted to hear them so badly. They were all the right things in his Southern drawl, and they terrified her. Not the words, really, but rather the choice she had to make about them. What would she do with them? She could accept them and do nothing, or she could be brave in her vulnerability. Theory could only get one so far; practice was required for the full experience.

She loosened an arm from around his neck and slid the free hand down until it rested on his belly. The head of his cock brushed the heel of her palm and she looked him in the eye.

"Can we try again?"

He shook his head. "I didn't say that to have sex with you."

She nodded and smiled softly. "I know. Can I make love to you?"

Max shuddered, resting his forehead against hers. He took a series of deep breaths and Ira hummed quietly, caressing his nape.

"Nobody's asked me that before."

"I thought you've been in love before."

"Yes," he confirmed, "I was still expected to lead, though."

"You will again," Ira said dryly. "I only have an idea of what I'm doin'."

Max chuckled deep in his throat, making her body thrum. "I think your ideas are *brilliant*."

Ira snorted and accepted his sweet kiss upon her mouth. His hand clasped hers and placed it upon his hardening cock. She was also getting wet again, the prospect of having this inside of her, of letting go completely and trusting Max to catch her.

"But if you make love to me, Ira," he said against her lips, "I want all of you. I want your cries and moans and grunts and cusses and caresses. I want your ugly faces and your O faces and your laughs. I want *everything*. Can you give that to me? Everything?"

"You mad greedy for someone I just met," Ira tried to tease, but his green eyes were serious, and his face was unsmiling. She started to ask what she'd get in return, but then decided against it. A large part of love was faith, and much less than that was quid pro quo. She had to have faith in what she felt for him. If she gave him all of her, she had to believe she'd get the same from him.

"Okay," she said, nodding. "I can give you that. I promise this time."

He nodded as well, burying his face into her neck. The wet, strong muscle of his tongue swiped her skin, making her shudder atop him and he moaned. His hand gripped her strong on her hips and he began to pull her into him.

"Get yourself ready for me, baby," he whispered into the hinge of her jaw. "Get yourself wet."

He sucked her skin and she felt blood rush to the spot. She gasped and squeezed his cock in reaction, her pussy growing incredibly damp at the sensation. This felt different from before. What had been gentle now had intent and purpose. Max had taken the kid gloves off and *oh*, how she adored the grown-up hands he touched her with now.

"Yes . . ." He groaned into her neck, then began a southern journey down her sternum to the space between her breasts. "Yes, ride me, baby, fuck. *Yes.*"

He guided her movements with his strong hands, movements she hadn't been aware she was making until she felt the head of him against her swollen clitoris. She hissed in a breath and tugged at the tendrils of his nape, her breath pooling against his temple.

Max drew a nipple into his mouth. Ira bucked sharply against him, the warm cavern of his mouth making her very wet. She firmed her lips into a kiss at his temple and dragged more firmly against his cock with her nether lips. His grip strengthened at her waist with a most delicious sensation.

Yet that wasn't nearly as delicious as the head of him piercing her.

Ira clasped his face into her breasts as she tried to slip more of him inside of her. It wasn't until his grip became too hard to ignore that she stopped.

"What's wrong?" she asked, pulling back to look at him.

His expression was wistful. "We need a condom, baby."

"Are you clean?" she asked, then immediately shook her head. That wasn't the point. He was a stranger, and they should wear condoms whether he was clean or not. That would be the responsible thing to do, after all.

"Yes," Max said. "I had my last checkup a few months ago and, remember, it's been more than a year since I've been with someone like this."

Ira nodded. "Okay." She still undulated her hips against him, still teased the head of his cock with her pussy.

"Ira," he said quietly, stopping her hips again. "Are you clean?"

"Yes," she replied. "I'm on birth control too."

He kissed her gently, more a press of lips as they shared breath. His iron grip on her hips eased. Ira's internal muscles clenched, wanting something to clamp around, and she brushed against his length again.

"Do you take your birth control regularly?"

Ira moaned, her brain not so lust-addled that she couldn't catch his drift. She also caught his cock in her hand again and brushed the head of him against her. His moan had her entire body twitching.

"Yes," Ira assured him. "I have an alarm on my phone and everything to make sure I take it at the same time every day."

Max shook his head but laughed lightly, coming back close to nuzzle into her. "You're really serious about it for someone who hasn't been sexually active."

"You try period cramps on for size, Max."

"Noted," he said against her cheek. "But we should really put on a condom, baby. No use courtin' trouble."

Ira did her best to suppress her wince, but she wasn't quite successful given how Max pulled back to look at her curiously. She avoided his eyes, climbing off of him instead. He was being responsible. He was absolutely right, though her pride had been pricked. She hid her face into a pillow and snorted. Not only had her libido been awakened, her biological clock had been too.

Great.

Max touched her back and she exhaled.

"I'm fine," Ira said. "I'm just . . . I'm gettin' caught up. Don't mind me."

She felt him kiss her right shoulder blade. "I always wear a condom, Ira. Client or no, I do my best to protect myself and my partner."

"You're a good man, Max," she said sincerely. "Like I said, I'm gettin' caught up in fantasy and being mad premature. It's just my pride. It's nothin' personal."

Max squeezed the fleshy bend of her waist and then left the bed, her body bouncing with the displacement of his departure. Ira curled in on herself, her body cooling from the hormones that had flooded her until sense returned. Max was right; there was no need to make reckless decisions in heated moments. Every choice had consequences, and fantasies never turned out the way reality actually did. She was grateful Max was considerate and kind. She'd seen horror stories walking in with venereal diseases or bellies full of babies that hadn't been planned for or wanted. That wouldn't be she come Wednesday morning.

Even as a small part of her wondered *what if*?

Sixteen

Standing in his bathroom, Max stared at the shiny foil packages in his hand with a frown. Condoms were a requirement whenever he had sex, one from which he never wavered or even gave serious consideration in forgoing.

Until now.

Despite the cool he'd just displayed, the thought had shaken him to his core. Only because of his prior experience in de-escalating matters and delaying his own gratification was he able to speak reason, but part of him wondered if he were just saying that because it'd always been in the script, or *could* he chuck it all out the window for her. All the reasons why one wore a condom were essentially irrelevant: they were both clean and she was on birth control. But wasn't that too fast to participate in an exclusive action when they were barely in a relationship? But they were in one, and Max realized Ira was feeling the urgency to pack an entire cycle of it into their brief weekend. Max couldn't rightly fault her for it, especially if she'd decided she would leave him firmly in the past once she boarded the train Monday morning.

His stomach dropped at the prospect, and he clenched the prophylactics in his hand. Max would survive the parting; he'd survived devastating separations before, after all. The void he carried inside of him would simply grow larger at Ira's loss, his world that much dimmer. Yet as he stared at his reflection in his brightly lit bathroom, Max realized that, unlike the other losses he'd suffered, he had a choice in how this one went—if at all. Ira hadn't insisted or pleaded her case that they *not* use protection, she'd simply put in the suggestion. Her odd reaction to his insistence was, in many ways, a far more honest one than his practiced placidness. He understood where she'd gone because, truth be told, he'd gone there as well.

"It's too soon," he whispered to himself, frowning fiercely at his reflection.

Or maybe the timing's just right.

His free hand trembled on his taut abdomen, and he closed his eyes. He'd said it, hadn't he? Ira was his harmony, with everything clicking into a place he hadn't acknowledged existing until her. She was a woman who wanted to love *him*, not his body or the wealth he could provide. Her nurturing spirit was a balm to his cracked soul; and as much as Ira had all but admitted she didn't think she deserved love, Max could admit he'd felt the same for much of his own life.

He opened his eyes wide, a revelation sinking into him, and he set the condoms back onto the counter before returning to the bedroom. Ira still lay atop the covers on her side, naked, the sounds of rolling ocean waves filling the room from the speakers. She didn't turn to face him, but he knew she wasn't asleep from the way she'd tensed at the sound of his footfalls. He said nothing as he climbed up on the bed and he kissed a plump buttock, his hand settling on the outer thigh of her top leg.

"I think I understand," he said against the curve of her hip. "What just happened. Why I accidentally hurt your feelings."

Ira shook her head and reached behind her to grasp his fingers. "You were right. I was being silly."

"No," Max insisted. "You weren't. You were taking my words to heart, and I was throwing your generosity back into your face. I'm sorry, Ira. I'm much better at dishing out wisdom than takin' it."

"Ain't we all?"

He chuckled into her hip, letting fring his tongue swipe at the taste of her. A little of the oil's flavor—nutty and slightly bitter—filled his mouth, but it couldn't mask Ira.

"I'm guessin' here, but I think you were intimating you'd be okay making love without a condom, right?"

She squeezed his fingers but answered affirmatively.

"And I think you were intimatin' that because you wanted to give me all of you without any barriers, even ones meant to keep us safe."

"Stupid, I know."

"No," he disagreed, now kissing the dip of her waist. "We talked about our histories and our health, and we both told each other we were clean, and you were on the Pill. You're a health care professional, Ira; you're not stupid. I'm in the business of providing companionship and giving women what they want within my own personal boundaries. I've had women ask about going bareback before and I never entertained the notion even after we had a histories talk that sounded like ours. But they wanted the experience of Me, not *Me*. You want *Me*."

At this, Ira flipped onto her back. Once she settled, Max situated himself between her legs and rested his chin on her pubic bone. Brows furrowed, Ira slid her fingers through the curls at the top of his head and he closed his eyes at her caress.

"I know you've been loved, Max. You're too good of a man not to have been."

The tears that started stinging his eyes were unanticipated, and he pressed his face into her abdomen. A woman hadn't gotten to the heart of a matter like this with him since his very first escorting experience. She'd been a much older woman—a foxy forty-something to his twenty. He'd fallen in love with her immediately even though all she'd wanted was a date to her high school reunion, a swan who'd been quite the rotund "geeky duckling" in her younger years. He'd doted on her, putting his true feelings into his actions, and she'd been receptive. She'd been his first, something that hadn't been a part of the initial arrangement, which had evolved throughout the night along with their feelings. He'd cried then, too, and she'd held him and told him he'd been the sweetest partner she'd ever had.

Max had never told the woman how much those words had meant to him. Shirleen McManus had given him the assurance he wasn't his father, nor did he have to be. He could touch a woman with care, treat her with reverence. His love wasn't obsessive or destructive. He was worth a good woman's touch.

"I used to get angry a lot," Max said quietly, "jealous. I didn't really play well with others, but I wasn't ever really violent—at least, not off the gridiron. I kept those thoughts inside and kept myself apart from people. I never dated in high school and barely in college . . . not until I met Shirleen McManus."

Max told her how Shirleen had been his first client, although nothing had been "official" at the time. He'd been Shirleen's server at a local diner in Montgomery where he went to college. She'd been a teller at the bank next door to the diner and she'd always eaten there. She'd flirted with him every time he served her, until one afternoon she'd propositioned him about being her date. The number she'd offered for his services had blown his entire mind, but the prospect of taking her out with her paying for everything was too enticing to ignore.

"You didn't feel used?" Ira asked, worrying the curve of his ear gently.

"No," he replied against her navel, "I showed her a good time and got paid to do it. Turned out, I was really good at being the perfect boyfriend. She's the reason I started Dream Dude LLC. She got me in touch with a tax guy, worked out a way to get me a loan with the bank—"

"In Alabama?" Ira asked, surprise in her voice.

Max chuckled. "Yeah. In fact, my loan officer became another client. But we never became intimate, mainly because she wanted me to take out her daughter. I was never intimate with her, either, because the daughter . . . well . . . she preferred girls."

"You were her beard?"

Max laughed again. "In a way. She liked guys, but she ended up falling in love with a woman bartender during one of our Dates. I was the go-between. That was one of my more fun experiences, actually."

"And what did the mama say?"

His smile faded. "Let's just say I switched banks."

"You could do that?"

"Yeah, by that time, I'd paid off the loan and then some. Shirleen had lined up more clients for me. So many lonely, unloved women in Montgomery, and it baffled me because the majority of them were *good* women. And I don't mean 'good' as in they didn't have any faults or anything. They were women who should've been at the top of anyone's list for a partner, but it was usually because of some superficial thing or another they weren't."

"Were they mostly older?"

"Yeah," Max said, resting his cheek on her belly. He smoothed his hands along her soft sides. "They're the ones with disposable money more often. Sometimes they used me to get back at their partners. Luckily, I looked too intimidating for any of them to actually come at me, but I've had tires slashed. Cars keyed. Shit like that made me raise my rates, but women still were willing to pay it."

"For a good time call . . ."

Max huffed and tickled Ira's sides, making her laugh and jiggle in response. "Damn straight. A safe, good time where you will be the center of my world for the allotted time. I had a lot of repeats in Montgomery. Was almost sad to go until Shirleen reminded me there are much bigger seas with much wealthier fishes. So, I skedaddled to NYC."

"Are you still in touch with Shirleen?"

"Oh, yeah," Max said, grinning. "She's still my registering agent in Alabama and she's a minority owner in the company. I love that woman."

"I can tell. It's all in your voice."

"I'll introduce you sometime."

"Really?"

The incredulity in her voice made Max's heart tight. "You wouldn't want to meet her?"

"I . . ."

He looked at her then and she was blinking up at the ceiling. Her breath shuddered out, as if she were trying to keep her emotions in check. His body relaxed and he kissed her navel, grinning slightly. "I think you'd probably want to thank the woman who taught me a lot about how to pleasure someone."

Now she snorted. "That confident in your skills?"

"You were moanin' somethin' fierce earlier tonight," Max reminded her, moving south along her body. He chose a trail down her left leg, starting at the bend where her hip and thigh met. Ira sighed sweetly, her fingers still gentle in his hair. Her pleased sigh made his length twitch to life, and he laved a long stroke in that bend.

"*Oh.*"

Max hummed his approval, pressing a full kiss there. Ira's hands became more insistent—only just—but she didn't guide him anywhere. Perhaps she was too nervous, too unsure, but she didn't have to worry about anything. It was a destination he definitely wanted to visit for a while.

"Just relax, baby," he crooned, moving even further down her thigh. It was generous and soft, and he couldn't wait to kiss every inch of it. Ira didn't know whether to grip him or let him loose by the way her hands kept clenching and unfurling. He smiled against her skin.

"Max."

He really liked how his name sounded rough with lust—Ira's lust. He was hard and burrowing a hole in his mattress, but his lips were caressing the softest place on earth. He took his strong hands to spread her wider, and her responding gasp was like an aria. He moaned, the smell of her arousal thick and heavy in his nose, and he wanted the taste of it on his tongue.

"I know you said you wanted to make love to me," Max whispered as he kissed up her other thigh. "But let me make love to you first, okay? It's still your birthday, and I promised."

"Max . . ."

"Shh," he soothed, licking the inside crease of her leg and hip, very near her now-glistening center. "Enjoy this, baby. I certainly will."

And with that, he kissed her right upon her hair-covered lips.

Seventeen

I ra tried to skitter away, but Max's hands were too strong upon her. He was going to make her accept his pleasure, and she was going to *like* it. Lord knew she did—too damn much. She was going to shatter, never to be whole again, and was *she* making those pitiful sounds? They sounded like "Yes!" and then "No!" and then "*Oh, God, F—!*" between very loud, high gasps. His tongue was *incredibly* thorough, not missing a crevice or a drop. When he hummed against her sensitive flesh, she answered him with a cry.

"Jesus fuckin' Christ," he muttered, right before sucking her swollen clit into his mouth.

She wouldn't even experience a full twenty-four hours of being thirty-one, because she was going to die. Sensations overwhelmed her, making her shudder violently even as she gripped the curls atop his head. Max hummed again, kissing her nether lips as if they were her mouth, stroking the outside of her thighs and hips with large, warm hands. Her nipples were so hard they hurt but she twisted them anyway, deciding to overload on sensation because *why not*? She was in too deep to stop now.

"You're gonna come for me, ain't you, baby?" Max asked once he'd deigned to leave her folds to speak. "Right in my mouth."

"*Nooo . . .*" she whined, horrified, yet intrigued by the prospect. His chuckle at her core had her whimpering and tightening her plush thighs against his ears.

"Yeah, you are," he replied, his eyes locked with hers as he slid a finger inside of her. She pulled him in greedily, yearning for the penetration, but it wasn't enough. She squeezed the digit harder with her internal muscles, her bottom lip finding its way between her teeth, and she arched her back into a bow. Max grunted, dropping a kiss to the top of her thigh, then her knee, before adding a second finger along with the first.

"Oh *yes.*"

He was massaging her inner walls with expertise, giving her an avenue to pleasure she didn't often use. Ira realized she rarely took her time during her intimate moments, too concerned with taking the edge off instead of basking in all the sensations she could feel. Max was forcing her to slow down and experience as much as she could, and he would make her feel everything possible.

"Baby, you're so tight and wet," he whispered, kissing her knee again. "I love how you grip me. Will you grip my cock the same way?"

Even Ira felt that surge of wetness at his words and she shuddered. Her pussy throbbed, wanting it, yearning for it. She glared at him when he laughed again, but her eyes drifted shut as his tongue swiped up a trail of moisture upon the inside of her thigh to where his knuckles brushed against her skin.

"I love the way you feel, baby," he continued to whisper with that low register, "the way you taste. I just might not let you leave come Monday. Got me *a-dick-ted*."

Ira snorted at that, not believing him for a second, then jumped and released a surprised giggle when light fingers brushed against her flank. Max drew up from between her legs with a shocked, yet pleased grin.

"I *so* love that you're ticklish!"

She grabbed his free hand, her eyes sharp. "Don't you dare!"

He laughed, kissing her belly. "I do, but not right now. I wanna make you scream too much to get you to laugh right now."

When he started up again, Ira certainly wasn't laughing. He was almost obscene with the way he kissed her, stroked her. He teased her clitoris with gleeful sadism, uncaring the pleasure was mounting too high too fast. She felt like a living flame, so hot she was amazed she hadn't singed the bedding. In contrast, Max's mouth and tongue felt cool, almost soothing, even as she careened closer to the brink of bursting.

Her heart pumped mightily. Ira wondered if he could see her clit pulse in time to it. He must not think that odd. This wasn't his first rodeo, after all, yet she didn't think she could hold on to this bucking bronco for much longer.

Her breathing became short, labored. Her vision misted at the edges and her face grew hot and damp. From tears of sweat, she wasn't sure, but the next time she opened her mouth, a sob so eerie escaped that it made her shiver.

She was floating now. Who'd known space could be so beautiful? She soared upon a warm cloud she couldn't see—only feel—and didn't want to come down.

"Ira?"

She sighed, the cloud rumbling about her. She liked the way it said her name, how comforted she felt.

"Baby."

Ira opened her eyes. There really *was* a Man on the Moon! He had green eyes, pale skin, rosy cheeks, and *incredibly* soft lips that quivered with his chuckles as he kissed her forehead.

"Come back to earth, baby," he cajoled. "Come on home."

Ira frowned, first hearing the birdsong that filled the room—Max's room—before Max's face sharpened into focus. He'd been the Man on the Moon and she'd never left the planet, at least not physically. She still felt weightless, though, and she reached up with her hand and cupped his cheek to further ground herself to reality.

He smiled and kissed the heel of her palm, his green eyes tender. "Welcome back."

Ira blushed and smiled even as she cringed. There was a cool rag upon her face that felt simply divine. "I passed out, didn't I?"

"Yeah," Max said with a nod, drawing a gentle swipe with the washcloth one last time before setting it on the nightstand. "Freaked me out for a second. I'd never had a woman pass out on me before."

"I'm sorry."

"Don't be," Max said, kissing her palm again. "I'll treasure that memory forever. Never knew I could love a woman so good she'd actually faint."

Ira rolled her eyes but laughed lightly, moving her hand from his cheek to drag her fingers through his hair. He closed his eyes, as if to relish in the caress, before opening them again. Then he kissed her, the press of his lips so gentle it caused her heart to flutter like butterfly wings. She felt his hardness against her hip, and she shifted slightly. He moaned into her mouth, and she opened hers to taste the sound. Max settled fully atop her, his big body a comforting weight, and she spread her thighs so he could fit in the cradle of them. He began undulating against her, his bare length against her still-damp center, and she sighed her pleasure.

"You still wanna?" His large-palmed hand slid down her sternum to her navel, then back up to a breast. He gathered the weight of it in his hand, his thumb brushing along the hardened tip of it. "Not afraid you might pass out again?"

"Think you can make me do it again, eh?"

He grinned, bending down to suck hard on her nipple. She couldn't help her gasp and sigh as he drew upon her. His rough, wet tongue licking upon the distended peak made her cream even more, especially when he switched to the other nipple to give it similar treatment. Her fingers tugged his curly brown locks as she offered more of her breast to him. She adored his mouth on her body and was amazed he seemed to adore it too.

The head of his erection grazed her nubbin, making her shudder. She whined when he lifted his head, but his eyes were so focused upon her it was all she could do not to shift her gaze away. His hand trailed down her plush belly to her core, and she felt his knuckles brush against her folds. He took himself in hand and increased the pressure of the drag, making her arch into it. His eyes remained locked on hers, and his hand cradled her jaw.

"You're not wearing a condom," she noted.

"I am not," he confirmed.

She frowned at him. "You said you didn't do this without a condom."

"I don't, typically, but there's nothing typical about this, Ira."

Her frown deepened. "I don't understand."

He gave a wry smile. "I don't, either, but the option you offered won't leave me be, even though it's one I'd heard countless times from many women."

Ira looked away from him to the nightstand. There, by the washcloth he'd set aside earlier, were condom packets. She picked one up and flipped the foil package between her fingers before looking at him again. His expression was neutral and remained so even as she gave it to him.

"You were right," she said. "We should do our best to protect each other."

"Yes," he said, his lips quirking. "I understand your earlier disappointment, though."

"Max."

"About gettin' caught up. I'm there, too, Ira. It's not about the condom, is it?" he asked, ignoring her staying tone. "It's never been."

She looked away from him and closed her eyes. He went still above her and didn't move again until she gazed at him once more.

"Why it'd been so easy to say no to previous requests to go without," Max continued while he opened the packet and pulled out the protection. "Why, even with Shirleen, I hadn't yearned to feel her walls close around my naked cock."

She watched him cover himself, the swollen head of him not so stark with the condom on, and she sighed brokenly when he swirled the head of himself in her wetness. The sensation was different, slicker, more artificial, and she mourned the loss of his immediate flesh upon hers.

"Just me?" Ira asked, pumping her hips in time with his strokes. Her walls tightened with the need for him to fill her, unable to withstand his teasing for much longer.

"Just you."

"Why?"

He kissed her instead of answering and began the first breach of his cock inside her slick channel. She already felt impossibly full and wanted to burst. She spread her legs wider, broken gasps pouring from her mouth against Max's lips as he sank further inside of her. She gripped his hip hard, feeling hot and humid and hurried to have him all the way to the hilt, but he kept his joining slow. When he was finally flush against her, he panted almost as heavily as she did, and his hand trembled where he cradled her head.

"Darlin'," he whispered shakily, his voice sounding awed to her ears. "*Oh*."

Ira clutched him, burying her face into his neck. This was an experience she'd despaired of ever having, and now it exceeded every expectation she'd given herself. She hadn't thought she'd cry, but the tears were coming, and she couldn't stop them. He didn't move beyond bracing himself on his forearms and brushing away her tears. He kissed her forehead, cheeks, nose, assuring her he was there, and it was all right to cry. She'd been so terrified of feeling so much, feelings she couldn't articulate or identify but were there all the same. Despite her pragmatism, she had to acknowledge that for her, this was a life-defining moment and she'd never be the same again.

"I'm not the first one to have cried like this," she said after a moment, her voice sounding as if she hadn't quite finished swallowing a jar of marbles.

"No," Max agreed, his forehead pressed against hers. "Are you okay?"

"I will be," she said, squeezing her legs and inner walls around him. "Are you?"

He kissed her knuckles and placed her fist to his heart. "Ira."

Now he sounded as if he'd swallowed a jar of marbles. She drew his face to hers with her free hand and kissed him gently, shifting her hips because she was getting hot, and he was getting heavy. He barely broke the kiss as he withdrew from her body then sank into her again, and the pace he began was leisurely, almost lethargic. Ira clung to him as he moved, each thrust making her gasp with pleasure and profound feeling. Max barely let his lips leave her face, and he murmured his ecstasy into her temple and cheeks. Her peak came much more quickly this time since she had no more defenses against it. She shouted his name and shuddered beneath him, and he followed a few strokes later with a final thrust and a whisper of her name.

Their breaths were harsh against the babbling brook that came from the speakers. Ira's face was wet with more tears; except this time, they weren't hers.

Eighteen

Max held Ira as if she were a favorite stuffed animal who would protect him from the dark. He'd had one in his youth, an incredibly large elephant one of his mother's boyfriends had won at the county fair for her, but he'd commandeered it and she'd let him.

The last time he'd seen the thing, its blue "skin" had turned purple because of all the blood.

He jerked awake and blinked hard at the dark ceiling, his arm loosening from around Ira, and sat on the edge of the bed. He did the breathing exercises his college therapist had taught him to do: inhale seven counts; hold seven counts; exhale seven counts. When he'd first started doing them, he would rush through the beats and then complain during the next session they weren't working. But cutting corners wouldn't cut it, and now he took his time. His heart started beating at a more sedate pace. He wiped away the sweat that had broken out along his hairline and relaxed his hands, which were clenched atop his knees. Only by sheer luck did he not jump when he felt small, warm hands upon his bare shoulders.

Ira.

He felt the adrenaline's effects fade at her touch. Her bare chest was soft and warm against his bare back, and Max closed his eyes when her arms wrapped around his neck in a hug.

"Everything okay?" she asked quietly, nuzzling the curve of his ear.

"Yeah," he said, nodding to make the affirmation stronger. "Bad dream." Even worse memory.

"Do you wanna talk about it?"

He pursed his lips shut. "I said I did earlier, but now, no."

She nodded. "Okay, then you don't have to."

"But I should."

She shook her head. "You really don't have to, Max."

"I wanna tell you. I need to."

Ira rested her temple against his, her arms making him feel very secure. Something about the Jackson women, because Gideon's hand holding his when he'd told her a rough sketch of what had happened had given him strength, emboldened him too. Ira's arms gave him the courage to unburden all.

"The short version is this: my father raped and killed my mother and I watched it all."

Ira inhaled sharply and her arms tightened around him. She didn't speak, and he couldn't for a few moments. Never had he been so blunt about it, and he felt lighter already.

"I hadn't known he was my father. I just remember my mama tellin' me to hide, so I did—right underneath the kitchen table. I was only four—not the brightest of boys—but I wasn't even noticed. There was a lot of yellin', then a lot of crashin', and then . . . silence. The silence was the loudest thing of all, really."

Well, maybe, the sound of his mother's body hitting the floor was the loudest, and the crack of her head against the linoleum floor still could make him jerk out of a dead sleep. His father's, "Get up, bitch!" had only been a derisive growl, that dusty, bloody boot kicking the prone body as if his mother had been contemptible roadkill. If his father had truly cared enough to bend down and check for a pulse, he would've seen Max, and Max didn't want to think of what would've happened then.

"I didn't want you to relive this," Ira whispered, her voice thick and her arms even tighter about him. "I'm sorry."

"You didn't do anything," Max said, though he couldn't stop his body shudders no matter how securely Ira tried to hold him. "*I* didn't do anything. It took me a long time to begin accepting that. I thought, maybe if I'd bitten him on the leg or something—"

"You would've been dead too."

Max nodded and shrugged. "Eventually."

"Max."

"I have a brother too," Max said after a moment, his breath shaky and inefficient. "Timmy. Tim. He's older. My father taunted my mother about him, sayin' he hated her for abandoning him, that he'd never want to see her, that his grandmother—*my grandmother*—would never let her see him again."

"Max."

"And my father was doing this while he was . . ." He couldn't continue, the memory of his mother's cries and his father's devastating words as he violated her too much for him to bear. The plan was to exhale, to continue the anti-anxiety measures he'd been taught; instead, a loud sob escaped him. Max folded upon himself, the force of the long-overdue purging emotions too much to keep him upright. He barely registered Ira letting him go, barely registered the bed bobbing with the redistributed weight. Max snatched in breath as if a vacuum was stealing it from the room until soft, cool hands brought his gasps to an abrupt stop.

"I'm here," Ira whispered softly, her nose pressed against his. "I'm right here, baby."

Max wanted to hug her but couldn't. His arms wouldn't move. Instead, he wrapped them around himself tighter as Ira whispered soothing, nonsensical words along the planes of his face. His cheeks were damp; though by the shuddering breathiness of Ira's voice, Max couldn't be sure it was because of his tears or hers. He hadn't meant to make Ira cry, but what had he expected? Perhaps the righteous fury Gideon had displayed, which had been so ridiculous Max had burst out laughing as he'd wrapped his friend into a grateful hug. Yet, Max hadn't sobbed, either, managing to keep his tone bland and level, as if he were well over the terror and anguish of that night. Of course, Ira—caretaking, nurturing Ira—would have a completely different response. Hell, deep in his heart, he'd counted on it, on the space she would allow for him to release the full brunt of everything he'd kept inside. The safety he'd felt with her, Max had never felt with anyone else.

Good Lord, how would he survive once she left?

"I'll be right back," Ira whispered against his forehead, and Max's stomach dropped to his toes when her presence and light moved away from him. She wasn't leaving; it was the dead of night, and they still had another full day to experience together. He hadn't miscalculated so spectacularly that she would leave him in the wreckage of this emotional fallout. Max closed his eyes, his breathing not nearly as wobbly as it'd been earlier, and looked up again when he heard Ira's footsteps reenter the bedroom.

"This'll make you feel better," she promised, seconds before a cool washcloth touched his face. He sighed and closed his eyes again, finally finding the wherewithal to wrap an arm around her plush waist. His embrace and her ministrations helped root him to the present. He wasn't under a table, listening to the last agonized sounds his mother would ever make. He wasn't squeezing his eyes shut and fervently praying the man wouldn't bend down and discover his hiding place. Nevertheless, he *was* still wondering about his grandmother . . . his brother. He had a brother and still lacked the courage to seek him out. If the boy had hated his mother, Max could only assume there would be no love lost for himself.

"Max."

He squeezed his eyes shut. Hot tears streaked down his cheeks. The terry cloth passed gently over his face.

"You don't really have to leave."

Ira said nothing. Max didn't press for a response. She finished wiping his face in silence then folded the washcloth and placed it on the nightstand. Max didn't let her go, resting his cheek against her chest when she was done, and basked in her tender fingers stroking through his hair. His hands began to caress her outer thighs, relishing in the soft smoothness of her skin. He turned his face to kiss the space between her breasts; her thumbs teased the tips of his ears. They heard a rare car drive down Biscayne Boulevard despite the late hour, the revving engine of an undoubtedly expensive luxury vehicle taking advantage of empty streets to test its horsepower.

Sighing softly, Max drew her closer until she straddled him. She came willingly, even going so far as to press her lips to his. He sighed into the kiss, his erection growing against the damp softness between her legs. She began to rock against him, little slow drags of her folds against his length, and he moaned. He needed her softness, her care right now. He needed to forget, to be reminded two people could touch each other with care and pleasure, not rage and pain.

Max blinked up at the dark ceiling as Ira's mouth moved down the column of his neck. Her hands glided up and down his biceps while his hands gripped the generous round globes of her behind, making her shift in a rhythm his hips liked. The tension in his body grew, but it felt too delicious to relieve right then. Ira gripped the flesh at the curve of his neck and shoulder with her teeth gently, tugging and making him gasp. He popped a buttock, smiling at her yelp and the way her flesh jiggled underneath his palm.

Max *hoped* she didn't leave.

As her mouth smoothed away the hickey she'd just gifted him, Max reached toward the nightstand and grabbed another condom. He pushed her back just enough so he could sheath himself, but he almost came when Ira plucked the package from his fingers. She took a few moments to stroke his hardness, to swipe at the moisture that had gathered at the tip and caress the veiny length of him. He tangled his fingers with hers and shared in her ministrations, his turn to sink her teeth in the fleshy slope of her shoulder while his other hand helped her grind upon a hair-roughened thigh.

"I wanna be inside you, Ira,'" he murmured against her shoulder. She shuddered and he gripped her hips harder, pulling her closer. "Put me inside. I wanna feel you come around me, baby."

"Max," she breathed against his cheek.

"I wanna feel what it's like to be loved right now," he whispered even more quietly, his throat trying to close over words he'd kept locked and buried in his heart for so long. But Ira deserved them. "I wanna feel what it's like to love in return."

Her lips were upon his temple as she sheathed him in the condom and slid down upon his covered length. Max rested his forehead along the column of her neck, shuddering hard in the aftermath of their joining. He'd had many intense lovemaking sessions, but none like this. He felt exposed, raw, one giant sore spot, and Ira was his salve. His salvation.

They were still uncoordinated, this only being Ira's second time having sex and Max too caught up in emotion to be of any help. But he'd arrived at the edge so quickly that he had to stay her hips atop him to get his bearings and some semblance of control. Ira continued to comb her fingers through his hair, and he continued to keep his face buried in her neck. She smelled like the oil, her, and him. It was his favorite fragrance ever. He needed to figure out how to bottle it to keep it with him always.

She was starting to grow heavy, and his thighs were becoming tired, but he never wanted her to leave this embrace, this intimacy. She was a grounding force in his life in this moment, a soft, generous woman who had so much to give and no one to receive her abundance. He wanted to be the recipient of her wealth, though. He wanted her to be his patron.

With a groan, Max fell back onto the bed, bringing Ira with him. Her unexpected squeal brought the first smile to his lips in a while, and he began to pump into her as he took her giggles into his mouth. He smoothed his palms along her wide back, finding the hills that formed the small of it and over the bountiful curve of her ass. Her ecstatic whimpers and moans drowned out his mother's terrified pleas. His enthusiastic grunts and groans shoved away his father's angry snarls. What remained was they and this moment; and although he could barely see her eyes locking with his, he could feel them. He cupped her cheek and she held his, taking each other higher and higher until they exploded with the release of everything they couldn't name—the words too paltry and insufficient to express the magnitude of what they felt.

Ira collapsed atop him, and he continued to hold her close. It was her turn to bury her face into his chest. It was his turn to rake his fingers through her hair.

He remained inside of her. She burrowed down as if making sure she couldn't let him go.

Nineteen

The throbbing between Ira's legs tugged her awake and she frowned. She'd read about this phenomenon in her romance novels, but for some reason, she hadn't thought it was an actual thing. But it was, and she groaned, stretching her legs to ease the soreness. Then she stared at the ceiling. The room was still dark thanks to Max's blackout drapes, but she suspected dawn had made her appearance hours ago.

Max slept on his back beside her, the covers bunched around his naked hips, his head turned away from her, one arm over his head with his hand facing up. It was too dim to see much of him, but that didn't stop her from reaching out and pressing her palm against his. He threaded his fingers through hers a moment later and turned his head to face her. He smiled first and she returned it.

"You're the most beautiful dark mass I've ever seen."

Ira burst out laughing, his companionable chuckles so deep they resonated within her. He pulled her hand to his lips and kissed her palm, then placed the bussed flesh upon his chest. She could feel the steady, relaxed pace of his heart underneath her hand, and she swiped her thumb along his nipple.

"How do you feel?"

"I thought that was my line," he teased, squeezing his fingers between hers.

"It's a mutual line," Ira compromised. "So?"

He sighed and rubbed his eyes with his free hand. "Weird."

Ira nodded. "That's fair."

She felt the bed shift, then his firm lips press against her shoulder. "I also feel very loved."

Her heart gave a mighty pump in her chest and her throat closed with unexpected tears. Max's mouth moved up her neck to the hinge of her jaw, his strong arms securing around her middle. He held her like this for a long moment and Ira closed her eyes to soak up the embrace. This was their last full day together. Tomorrow she'd be at the train station to leave this fantasy world and go back to her real life.

You don't have to leave.

Ira took a deep breath and closed her mind to that thought. She did have to leave. She wouldn't be irresponsible. But in this new-fangled world of mass communication, she and Max could talk, continue learning about each other, and see how strong these feelings could last in the real world. Ira thought hers pretty hearty. She wouldn't speak for Max, especially when he was still in a vulnerable state.

Excuse her, *weird* state.

Max's arms squeezed around her, making Ira's head jerk up so she could meet his eyes with hers. "You thinkin' real loud, baby. Care to share?"

Ira smiled softly and shrugged. "Just thinkin' how so much has changed for me."

His eyebrows rose. "Oh?"

She quirked her own eyebrow at him and pursed her lips. "I mean, aside from that."

He smiled, curling his fingers underneath her chin. "So, you never gave a mutual answer to the mutual line of questioning: how do you feel?"

She rested her forehead against his and sighed. "I feel weird too."

After they showered and dressed, Max took Ira to the famous S&S Diner, which was a fifteen-minute walk from his condo. The food was delicious, and the atmosphere was relaxed. The portions were generous, and the food was excellent—too excellent. They had to pack up the rest of their order because neither could eat any more.

"Perhaps we shouldn't have walked," Max said with a chuckle after a few blocks of silence between them. When they'd come earlier, the heat and humidity had been bearable. Now, they were completely soaked, and they still had several more blocks to go before they reached his condo building.

"We can test out that shower again," Ira placated, brushing away damp curls from his temples. "If I could, I'd pack up that shower and take it with me back to Moncks Corner!"

Max's smile wasn't as bright. "There's an idea."

Ira stopped, compelling him to do the same. She wrapped her arms around his waist and looked deeply into his eyes. "Would you prefer I pack *you* up and take you back with me to Moncks Corner?"

His smile softened, became more genuine, and he kissed her forehead. "That's an even better idea."

She trembled, unsure if he were serious or just continuing the teasing. Even though he was from Montgomery, Alabama, Moncks Corner was still too slow for the person Max was now. She sensed he required vibrancy and movement, not serenity and stillness. As for herself, Moncks Corner was much closer to her speed than Miami was, or even New York, where she learned Max kept his permanent residence during an earlier webcam chat. Ira liked quiet and peace, but she also liked Max a great deal too.

"Let's continue walking before we melt," Max said lightly, dropping one more kiss to her forehead before they continued on their way.

Once they reached his condo, they went directly to Max's shower, where he proceeded to clean every nook and cranny on Ira's body with a soapy washcloth and then undoing all that effort by following up with his tongue. She was a shuddering, incomprehensible mess by the time he was done, leaning dazedly against a slick wall while he washed his own body. She continued to thrum with the remnants of her orgasm when he approached, his hands cupping her face as he kissed her. She felt his sheathed erection dance along her nether lips, thanks to the condom he'd wisely brought into the shower earlier, and she slowly spread her legs. She was heavy and swollen for him; and when he slid home, they both sighed with pleasure.

Max grasped her abundant thigh and wrapped it around his waist, her new angle giving him the torque to thrust more deeply than before. His other hand had wrapped around both of her wrists above her head as he kissed and nosed her face. His thrusts were measured, deliberate, and Ira couldn't help her shudders or gasps. Her leg felt weak, and she began sliding down the wall, but Max gave a mighty pump that kept her upright. He remained there, buried to the hilt with his eyes intense upon her face. Ira lifted her chin to kiss him, gentle in contrast to the force of his earlier thrusts. Max deepened this, too, his tongue stroking hers, his teeth tugging at her lips. Soon, his tongue and cock began stroking in the same rhythm, and Ira couldn't do anything but take it.

"Come for me, baby," Max commanded against her lips after a moment. "Come all over my cock. I love the way you squeeze me, Ira. Squeeze me now."

He laced his fingers through one set of hers and then thrusts so deeply his erection dragged against her swollen clitoris. She cried out and fell apart, her voice reverberating in the stall and making her ears twitch. Max followed directly with a guttural groan that had her internal muscles clenching around his length in response.

He pressed his face against her temple, his fingers clamping hers so tightly she hissed with discomfort, but she didn't make him let go. Instead, she tilted her head against his and hummed comfortingly, providing an anchor he so obviously needed.

The water turned cold. The shower's comforting humidity became frigid. With a grunt, Max withdrew fingers and cock from her to turn off the rain showerhead, and it was abruptly quiet in the stall. Ira looked at him, her bottom lip caught between her teeth, as she watched Max stare at her with an unreadable expression. His fingers held the full condom around his flagging length. To her dismay, she found herself growing wet again. She groaned, hiding her face in her hands.

"What's wrong?" he asked, his deep voice filling the stall with delicious resonance.

"You're too fine," Ira groused. "I want you again."

He laughed, though not unkindly. "Oh good, I thought it was just me."

She peeked at him through her fingers. "Really?"

"Baby, if I had my way, you'd be on your back for the rest of the day."

Ira's mouth dropped open and her eyes widened, and this time his answering grin was very naughty.

"Greedy, greedy, greedy!" Ira chanted, finding the strength to leave the shower stall. She gave Max a wide berth as she did.

"Yeah, I am," Max called behind her.

"I wasn't talkin' 'bout you," Ira returned, her own naughty grin forming at his strangled exclamation.

Despite the shower they'd just taken, Max and Ira walked the ten minutes it took to the Pérez Art Museum Miami, which overlooked Biscayne Bay. It housed contemporary art among multiple stories, although to Ira's eyes, the architecture itself was part of the art. There were hanging flora on the outside rafters, as well as sitting areas on the wood patio surrounding the building. Ira snapped so many pictures with her phone that her battery was hanging on by a thread before they'd even gotten inside.

"I suppose you want me to take the rest of the pictures," Max drawled once they entered the museum. To their immediate left was a funky installation full of bold colors that Ira wanted to document for posterity.

"Please," Ira said, squeezing his arm. "If you'd be so kind."

Like a dutiful attendant, Max took every picture Ira requested, which were numerous because there wasn't an exhibit Ira didn't like. As with the botanical gardens yesterday, Ira was astounded by the sights she saw. Many of the installations weren't beautiful per se, but they were striking and made one think. The art was modern and evocative, sometimes even provocative, and it was a great contrast to the gardens' traditional beauty.

After about an hour, Ira was ready to go; or rather, her stomach. Max arched an eyebrow at its growling and Ira rolled her eyes.

"I thought you'd said you were full at breakfast," Max teased.

"It's lunchtime now. Feed me, Dream Date," Ira commanded.

Chuckling, Max linked their fingers together and they walked back to his condo. After another quick shower—this time without the extracurriculars—they reheated the leftovers from yesterday's lunch and ate in the kitchen. It was too hot and humid for the balcony this time. They sat in robes, a terry cloth one for Max and the robe from her brand-new lingerie set for Ira, and they spoke about everything but Ira's impending departure the next morning.

"Why don't you live in Miami full time? You really like New York that much better?"

Max shook his head and shrugged. "More opportunities in New York. And it's a better hub city than Miami. Easier to get to and from, especially overseas."

"You have overseas clients?"

"Not yet," Max said, "but I'm working on that. Gideon's really been pushing to have a London office, but I've not done my due diligence about that yet. I'm not sure about wanting to expand internationally. I'm not even sure if I want to continue doing this."

Ira blinked in surprise. "Really?"

Max shrugged. "I mean, full-time. I want to do something else. I'm not sure yet, but the day-to-day operations for Dream Dudes aren't as fun as it used to be for me."

"Do you miss being a Dream Dude?" Ira asked. "Maybe you stopping that part of it has made you feel bored?"

He smiled and shook his head. "It was good for my twenties. Now I'm interested in roots, the future. I do have Dudes who are in their thirties and forties, but they either aren't ready or don't want to be tied down. They're excellent at what they do, but I want to be one woman's Dream Dude."

His smile remained, but his eyes held no humor as they gazed upon her. A thrill ran through Ira, and she clutched her hands in her lap underneath the table. She would not ask the question that burned her tongue, if he'd found the woman for whom he'd be her Dream Dude. She wasn't strong enough to hear the answer she suspected; wasn't brave enough to let him be hers beyond these next eighteen hours.

Max nodded and drank the rest of his mimosa, though his eyes remained on her. "No thoughts?"

"Too many."

"Stop thinking, then," Max suggested. "Start living instead."

Twenty

“**O**h, oh *yes.*”

"Hey, watch that mouth, baby. There're children about."

Ira's eyes widened, then she buried her face into his damp neck and giggled, making Max grin and hold her close to him. They were in the pool deck's small hot tub, having commandeered it after a pair of ladies had gotten out of it fifteen minutes earlier. At the start of their trip to the pool area a half an hour ago, they'd cuddled on one of the chaise lounges near the infinity pool underneath a large umbrella to protect him from the sun's rays. He'd read softly to Ira, *Persuasion* by Jane Austen, more to share in her serenity than anything else. She'd been silently reading it to herself while he'd observed children from a family of five frolicking in the water, their father tossing his children in the water while the mother looked on fondly from the pair of chairs they'd used for their pool trip's home base. Max had absently slid his hand from

Ira's waist to her belly as he'd watched them, making Ira pause in her reading and look at him curiously.

He'd offered to read aloud so she wouldn't ask him what was on his mind.

It'd also been his idea to get into the hot tub once it'd become available. Ira had hesitated, unsure about un-donning her cover-up to reveal her bathing suit to everyone. She hadn't even let him see it, which Max had thought silly since he'd seen her nude several times beforehand, but it wasn't his place to judge Ira, or any woman for that matter, about her hang-ups.

"You've got to be a little sore," he'd said along the line of her jaw, Austen forgotten in favor of convincing Ira to join him in the hot tub. "It'll feel good, I promise."

"You'd say anything," Ira had muttered.

"Nothin' but the truth, baby," he'd promised. "Come on."

Max held Ira closer as he remembered her finally revealing her bathing suit. It was a black two-piece with a halter bust and high briefs at the bottom. Her round tummy poked out between the top and bottom of the suit, which had compelled Max to kiss her belly button. She'd snickered, relaxing from her nerves of exposing herself in public, and Max nuzzled her stomach in commendation of her bravery.

"Max, the children," Ira had chastised, and Max had scowled as he lifted his head from her.

"Fine, I'll keep it PG," he'd agreed. "You owe me, though."

Max was upholding his end of the bargain, keeping his hands in safe areas as the heated hot tub relaxed their aching muscles. Even he was tight in places he hadn't anticipated. Ira, however, was being a little minx. The comforting swipes of his chest with her hand hadn't broken the water's surface in a while. In fact, those swipes were now sliding underneath the elastic of his swim trunks to stroke his burgeoning erection. Max let his head fall back, the combination of the gurgling water and her grip too much to bear.

"Behave, seriously," Max murmured. He couldn't kiss her, or else they'd give that family of five and everyone else quite the show.

"Those heffas are still lookin' at you like you a tall drink of water. They can stay parched for all I care."

Max looked to his right, where the pair of women really was gazing at him as if he could quench their thirst, this when each wasn't looking at Ira with jealous confusion. They were typical Miami ladies: bronzed, trim, conventionally perfect. They'd look right at home on a billboard or fashion magazine cover.

When Max had led Ira by the hand into the hot tub, the women's gaping expressions and loud whispers had made Ira hide underneath the churning water in a corner of the tub. Max had frowned at Ira's reaction, then at the ladies, who'd pasted on becoming smiles for his benefit.

"Ladies," he'd greeted tersely, then entered the water himself, rolling his eyes at their reaction. Ira had popped her head back up when he reached her, her eyes darting about the rim of the hot tub.

"They're gone," he'd told her.

"Good," Ira had muttered. "I was about ready to go off!"

Max grinned at that memory, and the ladies who were in his line of vision smiled in return. He sighed and gazed back at Ira, who snorted her own amusement.

"*Parched!*"

"You're enjoying this, me being coveted like a piece of meat to a pack of hyenas," Max grumbled, lifting her in the water so her legs wrapped around his waist.

Ira laughed and hugged his neck with her free arm, her occupied hand still caressing him. "I'm the one who's being quenched and fed, so you're damn right."

He was hard as a rock now. "I'm a buffet, then?"

"Tastiest one I've ever had."

He chuckled and kissed her cheek, bucking his erection into her hand. "Voracious and salacious. I'm liking this side of you, Ira."

They remained in the tub for another fifteen minutes, mainly just holding each other as the water continued to soothe them. The children's squeals and the Miami breeze added to their peaceful experience. Even Ira's teasing had become therapeutic in a way, her own version of an erotic massage where she brought him just short of the edge, only for him to float down before ramping him up again. Though it was her hand upon him, he set the pace, enjoying the tension she caused and trusting she wouldn't make him lose it in such a public setting. There was a thrill at the possibility of getting caught, however. He was sure the pool attendant wasn't completely unaware of what they were doing, nor were the ladies ignorant, considering the pair had been watching them like hawks since they'd entered the hot tub. But Max was willing to indulge Ira's naughty side up to a point, especially when she would be paid back with an abundance of interest once they returned to his condo.

"Gotta stop now, or we'll be banned from the pool for life," he warned, grasping her wrist gently.

She kissed his cheek with soft lips. "Wouldn't want that, would we?"

Groaning, Max set her away from him and tried to think of something that would make his erection disappear. Watching Ira talk to the kids' mother and coo over the little ones didn't help initially; but then he remembered she would be gone twenty-four hours from now, and that got him good and soft.

"Wait here," Max snapped with more irritation than he'd intended. Both women looked at him with shock and he shook his head, kissing Ira's cheek in apology. "Just mean, I'mma get the towels so you ain't shiverin' when you get out."

"It's warm, Max," she reminded him, but her smile was gentle and accepting.

"Let me be a gentleman, baby," he said, winking at the mother. "I'm tryin' to show off for your new friend here."

The mother giggled and Ira rolled her eyes as he climbed out of the hot tub and went to their chaise. He gathered up the two pool towels the attendant had given them earlier, wrapping one around his waist before returning to the hot tub. The mother had two of her children clinging to her knees now, one of them grinning widely at Ira while the other played peek-a-boo with his mother's hip. The grinning child looked up at him when he approached, and Max smiled as well.

"Hi, there."

She now played peek-a-boo with her mother's other hip.

"Losing your touch, there, Max," Ira teased. "Women usually flock to you, not flee."

He shrugged and held out a hand to her, tucking the towel underneath his free arm. "As long as you don't flee, I'm good."

"¡Usted gana, chica!" the woman said with a laugh. "¡Usted gana!"

Ira smiled, but it was clear she didn't understand what the woman had said. Max shook his head on Ira's behalf and replied.

"Yo gano," he answered, drawing Ira close when she was fully out the pool and wrapped the towel around her. "Ella es mi regalo."

The woman laughed and squeezed her babies to her. "Bueno, you two have a lovely afternoon!"

"Goodbye," Ira said and waved at the young ones, who smiled and waved in return as they went back to their chairs. She then looked at Max curiously. "What did you two say?"

He shrugged, tightening the towel about her. "She said you win, and then I said I win and you're my gift."

Even though he couldn't see it, he knew she blushed by the way she shyly averted her eyes. "Actually, you're *my* gift."

"Semantics," Max mumbled, dropping a kiss to her nose. "Ready to go?"

"Yeah."

They gathered their belongings, Ira putting back on her cover-up while Max turned in their towels. That done, they returned to his condo where they took yet another shower, both of them laughing at the frequency with which they'd cleaned themselves today.

"You have the most relaxing hands," Ira said on a moan.

Max smirked, her sudsy hair so soft beneath his fingertips. He liked the feel of her short curls underneath his palms. It was as soothing for him as it was for her.

"Are you sure my conditioner will be okay?" Max said.

"Yeah. I also have some coconut oil that I'll put on later," Ira said, dipping her head underneath the shower's spray. "I'mma miss those hands come tomorrow."

Max winced at the casual, almost off-handed way Ira made the comment, but she didn't see since her eyes were closed under the water's onslaught. He finished washing her hair, his jaw clenched and his nostrils flaring, then he stepped underneath the spray as soon as Ira moved away.

"Max?"

He didn't answer, letting the shower drum the tension out of his shoulders. His hands were braced against the stall, and he glared at the water droplets on the wall. He didn't jump when he felt her arms band around his shoulders, but some of his rigidity did ease when her breasts and belly pressed against his back.

"Are you okay?"

"No," he answered honestly, "but I will be."

She rested her cheek against his shoulder blade and stroked his taut belly. "I'm sorry."

Max sighed, taking one hand from the wall to hold hers against his stomach. "I know, baby."

They didn't dally long in the shower, but they were certainly more subdued now than they'd been earlier.

They dressed in finery, Ira wearing a beautiful strapless canary dress while Max donned a plum button-down shirt with slate-gray slacks and jacket. Max was Ira's balance bar as she put on her three-inch black heels, and he was a good sport about taking a selfie in front of his full-length mirror. He hid behind her as best he could because she should be the focal point of any picture they took. She looked like ebony and sunshine, bright and pineapple smelling and delicious. That the selfie she'd taken, catching him with his nose atop her head and his eyes closed, looked loving instead of creepy was providence because he'd definitely been smelling her hair.

Ira snorted at him, knowing exactly what he'd been doing, and put her phone in her clutch. "You're lucky you're so damn photogenic."

"If that ain't some pot-kettle rhetoric right there," Max said with an arched eyebrow.

She grinned at him and held out her hand. "Let's go, gorgeous."

He flushed and took her hand. "What's it with you stealin' all my lines?"

Ira laughed and squeezed his fingers. "Quicker on the uptake, I suppose. But I'm sure you have plenty more up those beefy sleeves of yours."

"I ain't beefy."

"You're a regular beefcake, Max. It's okay."

"If you'd seen me back in college, you woulda called me a porterhouse."

"That's what I'mma order when we get to the restaurant."

"You mean you haven't had enough yet?"

Ira frowned, initially not understanding his meaning. But when she did, she gasped and slapped his right biceps lightly with the back of her hand. "Max Worthington!"

He cackled as they waited for the private elevator to reach their floor. "Ain't all as quick as you thought, hmm?"

He let her ignore him until they were both alone in the elevator. Then he pulled her back to her front and let his lips graze her ear. "Don't worry, baby. I aim to keep you good and fed and satisfied for as long as you let me."

And he had a few hours to convince her he meant beyond tomorrow too.

Twenty-One

Luckily for Ira, the restaurant was in the same building as Max's condo, so they didn't have far to walk. While her shoes made her legs look absolutely fabulous, the heels were too precarious for Ira's liking. She could hear Gideon chastising her about not practicing walking in the shoes, but Ira shoved the voice out of her head. Truth be told, she probably wouldn't have worn them at all if not for the lust that had filled Max's eyes when she'd modeled the outfit earlier that evening. Besides, if she tripped, she knew Max would catch her, and any excuse to be in his arms was a welcome one.

The host was pleasant as he led them to their table. They took up a corner of a booth that faced the window, giving them a view of Biscayne Boulevard. There wasn't much traffic, considering it was a Sunday night, and the jumbo screen on American Airlines Arena flashed with beer and sports advertisements. The live DJ played an old-school soul mix that had Ira bouncing in her seat to the beat, her fingers snapping underneath the table as Stevie sang about part-time lovers.

Sitting catty-corner to him, Ira met Max's eyes, and his lips lifted with a half grin. So, the quasi-irony didn't escape him either.

When their server arrived, he gave Max a large smile and a hearty slap-handshake, the pair speaking in rapid Spanish. Ira smiled and chuckled to herself. This was the second time in as many hours she was completely lost in conversation. Most of the little Spanish she knew was relegated to medical terms like enfermo, fiebre, and ¿Dónde le duele? while pointing to various body parts. Luckily, they always had a bilingual intake nurse on call, but Ira suspected she should really get serious about taking Spanish lessons.

"Dios, but all her relations are fine, ain't they?"

Ira blinked, getting out of her head and into the present conversation. "We're back to English?"

The server blushed and ducked his head, placing a hand to his chest. "Lo siento, that was rude of me. I'm Guillermo, a friend."

Guillermo held out a lightly tanned hand that Ira accepted. His hold was strong, his skin soft, and she grinned despite herself.

"Okay, that's enough!"

Guillermo arched an inky eyebrow at Ira, tossing his head toward Max. "He said that with Gideon, but they weren't dating either. *You cannot hoard all the beautiful women, Maximus!*"

Ira laughed, both at Guillermo's mock stern rebuke and the name. "Maximus!"

Max glared at the server but then turned sheepish eyes at Ira. "That's my full name."

"Really?"

Now he narrowed his eyes at her. "I was born before *Gladiator* came out, may I remind you."

"I mean, yes, but . . . that's . . ." she trailed off with a giggle. "I actually think it suits you."

He arched an eyebrow at her. "Really?"

"I mean, you *do* entertain me."

She watched Max inhale deeply, his nostrils flaring. She'd seen that expression several times already, usually right before he got her naked and writhing in his hold. Ira dropped her face to hide her burgeoning grin, and she didn't even look up when she heard Guillermo snort.

"Yep. She's definitely Gideon's cousin!"

"We'd like water and the house wine, please," Max rumbled, and Ira kept her gaze averted until she felt his presence next to her.

"I can't wait to 'entertain' you more tonight," he whispered, kissing her earlobe after a quick tug before returning to his seat.

Ira's body hummed throughout the entire, delicious dinner. Her steak was seasoned and seared to perfection, and she shot Max naughty looks every time she took a bite of it. Max didn't play fairly himself, however, licking his full lips after every sip of wine and each bite of his pork chop.

"Not gonna share?" Ira asked, looking longingly at the thick slab of marinated meat on his plate.

Max didn't look up, simply cutting his meat. Ira shrugged and started back on her steak when a pork-filled fork entered her line of vision.

"Seriously?"

"If you want it, come and get it."

Her eyes trained on his, Ira leaned her head forward and bit air. Her teeth clattering together made her wince, and Max's chuckle at her expense almost made her cuss. She didn't want a bite that badly, so she went back to her steak.

"Giving up that quickly?"

"I ain't chasin' after no pork, *Maximus*." She made a grand show of savoring her steak, going so far as to gather the mashed potatoes with it and eating the bite with a decadent moan.

"No, no sex sounds at the table."

She almost choked on her food. "Max!"

"No O-faces either," he continued with a glower at her plate, not stopping when Guillermo approached their table with his own frown.

"Something wrong with the food?"

"She likes it too much!" Max snapped, pointing accusingly at the plate.

At first Guillermo looked at him, then the plate, in bewilderment. Meanwhile, Ira ate another bite and did a little pleased shimmy. Guillermo smiled, then chuckled, then placed the back of his hand to his mouth to keep from guffawing flat out. He walked away like that, and Ira didn't bother hiding her own giggles.

"Some friends y'all are," Max mumbled, cutting into his pork chop once more.

It took Ira a solid minute of laughing into her napkin before she could completely swallow and start on another bite of her steak.

"I'm never gonna hear the end of this, am I?"

Ira snickered. "From me or Guillermo?"

"*Gideon*," Max complained. "I'm sure Guillermo texted her immediately after *that*!"

"You deserve to get dragged for acting like a dick," Ira said flatly. "And for teasing me with that pork chop."

"I'm possessive of your love sounds, Ira. I'm not gonna apologize for it."

She had to set her utensils down at that, the declaration making her unexpectedly hot. She chanced a glance at Max and saw the look of triumph on his face.

He was an asshole.

"You're not even trying to use an inside voice," Ira managed after a moment and a healthy sip of her iced water.

"Not really, no, considering damn near every other server and busboy keeps looking at you each time you put a bite of food in your mouth."

"They aren't," Ira said, scoffing.

"They are," Max insisted. "You haven't noticed because, I think, you're purposefully oblivious to the attention you get and because you're with me and you have food in front of you."

Ira frowned at him, setting her utensils down again. "What does *that* mean?"

"Which part?"

She didn't buy his curious expression for a moment. "You made me sound like an ignorant, greedy woman!"

He genuinely looked surprised and confused. "That wasn't my intent, at least not about the food and me. You're too respectful to let your eyes stray, and you enjoy your meals. Every time we've eaten together, you've been supremely focused on me and the food. That's—that's a great thing, Ira. It makes a partner feel good to command all of your attention like that."

It took a moment for Ira to register the words; yet when she did, she shrank in her seat, immediately chastened. "I'm sorry."

He cocked his head at her. "That was an unexpectedly sore spot. Who made it tender for you?"

Ira shook her head, her appetite disappearing at her unwarranted reaction. "I'm such an idiot."

A gentle finger upon her chin made her squeeze her eyes shut at their unexpected sting, and she took a deep, bracing breath before meeting Max's eyes.

"When the company's not good, I suppose you focus completely on the food, huh?"

Her cheeks burned, but she nodded. Max was clever and observant; it wouldn't have been difficult to guess that. And by the understanding that appeared in his eyes, he'd guessed something else too. But Ira would be brave and confirm verbally.

"When the conversation fizzled, at least there was the food. If there were any monitors playing a game or a TV show, I'd watch those too. I've actually been called inattentive more times than not."

"You were quick with your defense and outrage," Max said with a nod. "I didn't mean to offend you."

"I know. You were trying to compliment me."

"He's bad at doing that," Guillermo said when he approached their table, refilling their water glasses.

"Barely has a kind word for me despite my excellent service."

Max pursed his lips together, his expression stony. "I thought my tips said more than enough."

Guillermo arched an eyebrow and held up an index finger. "*Touché*. Can I get you anything else?"

"A to-go box and the dessert menu for me please," Ira said.

"Same."

"If you're not done—"

"The sooner we're done here, Ira," Max said, not bothering to complete that thought.

Ira barely registered Guillermo had left with a sharp turn to fulfill the requests, Max's green eyes snagging hers until she couldn't bear the weight of his gaze any longer. Looking down, Ira inhaled and exhaled deeply, her insides trembling. She downed the heretofore untouched glass of wine—a red—and licked her lips to capture every drop. She then jumped when Max's fingers interlocked with hers.

"Look at me, baby."

Max had slid closer to her, a fact she'd registered a while ago because his presence was so overpowering. When she finally did, his features were soft and open. He kissed her knuckles and smiled.

"I still have at least another ten hours with you," he murmured against her skin. "I want them to be pleasant, okay?"

"I told you I was good at self-sabotage," Ira said with a wry grin.

"Yes," Max said, chuckling, and he kissed her knuckles again. "But you ain't gonna thwart me, Ira. This parting's gonna hurt something fierce, but let's not hurry that moment along, okay?"

Max was completely right. There was no guarding against the pain that would come once he dropped her off at the train station, no way to prepare for it. She might as well fully enjoy every moment she had with him now.

Guillermo arrived just then with a paper bag full of their leftovers and a leather-bound menu, presenting it to her.

"He's stopped being mean?" Guillermo asked Ira in a stage whisper.

"I was the unpleasant one," Ira admitted with a self-conscious shrug.

Guillermo clucked his tongue and shook his head. "He still must've done something."

"Just be wonderful," Ira said, looking at Max with bright eyes. He squeezed her hand again.

"We want the desserts to-go too," Max said, his gaze never once leaving hers.

"Okay, what would you like?" Guillermo said, his tone so professional Ira looked up in surprise. Guillermo grinned at her. "I like to chat, but I don't think your man's up for any more chatting."

Her stomach swooped at the possessive that would only belong to her for a few more hours. "I'd like the cheesecake, please."

"The warmed chocolate-chip cookie," Max replied, "no ice cream."

"Got it," Guillermo said, taking the menu from her; and with a soft smile, he went to fulfill their order.

The DJ was still on point, now playing classic Boyz II Men, a slow jam that made her sway. Max stroked her fingers and tilted his chin in the direction that Guillermo had gone.

"He applied to be one of my Dream Dudes," Max revealed, "Gideon had scouted him, said he was charming."

"He is," Ira said. "He's been an entertaining server."

"Yes, but as charming and as much of a flirt as he is, he wasn't Dream Dude material."

"Why?"

"He just wanted to have a good time," Max said with a "what can you do?" shrug. "And, as you've experienced, these Dates can run the gamut. Also, he was too focused on the physical and not on anything else."

"He's young," Ira said.

"Yeah, but he's a good kid. I think this type of service has really helped him learn how to interact with all sorts of people. If he applied again, I'd probably accept him."

Ira nodded. She could see that about him now, although she was intrigued Gideon had suggested him for a Dream Dude in the first place. Then again—

"Exactly what does Gideon *do* in relation to Dream Dude LLC?"

Max grinned at the question. "Exactly what I said: she scouts Dudes for me. Working in the fashion world, she has access that I couldn't begin to reach. Besides, many men aren't comfortable with another man asking them to be random women's dates."

"And how did she become someone who did that?"

Max now drained his glass of wine. "Gideon used to be one of my clients."

Twenty-Two

Max wasn't quite sure what he'd expected Ira's reaction to be but, the slow stretch of her lips into a smile hadn't been among them.

"Just for Dates, not for anything more," she said matter-of-factly.

Max frowned and nodded. "Yes."

Ira's smile widened and she nodded as well. "She would've never given you my number if there'd been something deeper between you two, not even to hook me up with anyone else—at least, not alone. She would've used you two as an example of what *I* could have if you'd just let her lead the way."

Max had to smile at that. "You really know your cousin."

"So do you," Ira teased, "I see that recognition in your eyes."

"She's nurturing, too, just in a more aggressive, annoying way," Max said with an endeared chuckle.

"How did you two meet, anyway?" Ira asked, finishing her glass of wine.

"She answered a modeling ad I'd put out," Max said. "She was already giving her spiel before the casting agents could reject her outright, and we both know they would've."

Ira nodded, her expression solemn. "You would've let them?"

Max shook his head. "Though she wasn't the look I'd had in mind, there's no denying your cousin is a gorgeous woman."

Ira smiled again. "Once she started embracing all of those curves she had, it was a wrap."

Max's smile faded. He really wanted to embrace *Ira's* curves right now. He only had a few hours left where he could do so. As he watched her own smile fade, Max accepted the fact it was time to get the check.

He caught Guillermo's eyes a few tables away and the other man nodded imperceptibly. Ira was looking out the dark window, her rounded profile so lovely to his eyes. Unable to help himself, Max pressed his lips along the ebony stretch of her throat. Even despite the savory smells of the steakhouse, her pineapple scent made his mouth water for more.

"Max," Ira said with a shaky sigh.

"I'm gonna love you so good when we get upstairs, baby."

"Can you wait until we get there?" Ira asked in a strained whisper.

"Please?" Max heard Guillermo add from behind. "My manager's lookin' a little leery."

Max paid the check, and the to-go bags were ready in seeming moments after that. They said their goodbyes to Guillermo, Max ignoring Guillermo's pointed look, and Max ushered Ira out the restaurant with a hand to the small of her back. He felt her shudder, saw the slight stutter-step she gave as she navigated around waiting patrons at the front, and he pressed himself against her to steady her. If she felt his erection at her back, then he wouldn't apologize for it like he usually would've. He'd given her ample warning of what he was going to do, and she hadn't said no.

But she'd said to wait until they get upstairs; and while that hadn't been a "no," it was a definite "not right now," so he backed away to give her some breathing room. He watched her shoulders relax, and her bright smile to the restaurant attendant as he opened the door to let them leave indicated her relief at Max's reprieve.

Max tangled their fingers together in a sort of compromise. He wouldn't be all up on her, but he wouldn't let her completely go either. His urgency for her would be appeased very soon, and she wasn't in the mood for playful teasing. He couldn't blame her. Teasing meant they had more time than there was. Max felt as if he'd pop with frustrated longing if he didn't get her into his arms soon.

They reached the elevator, and they were both relieved they didn't have to share it. In the privacy of the contraption, Ira felt comfortable enough to snuggle against him now. Max kept her close and his hands in appropriate places. There were security cameras, after all, and he'd do nothing to embarrass her like that.

However, as soon as the doors opened to his condo's vestibule, the leash he had on his control slackened dangerously.

"Get out," he ordered gruffly, his voice as deep as the night sky.

Ira left the elevator on visibly trembling legs, forced to brace herself on the small table in the vestibule. Max spun her around, letting the to-go bags and his blazer that he'd carried in the crook of his arm drop to the floor. He hiked her legs high upon his waist as he rested her ass on the small table, kissing her hard like he'd wanted to all night. He tasted the remnants of her dinner and her, groaning at the savory sweetness that hit his tongue.

"Now," he grunted into her mouth, already gathering the skirt of her dress to bunch at her waist. Moments later, his hands found the elastic band of her panties and he jerked the fabric down. Ira was no less busy, her hands fumbling with the zip, button, and buckle of his slacks and belt, and he did a shimmy to drop everything to his ankles, making her smile. He tasted that smile as he ground himself against her, feeling her incredible dampness against his rigid hardness, and he groaned when she tugged his underwear down over his erection. It bobbed free, the air cool against the pre-come on his swollen head, but the liquid heat between her thighs warmed him right up.

"I'm comin' in, baby," he whispered against her lips. He grasped his erection and teased the head of it along her folds. Her inner thighs scalded the backs of his fingers deliciously. When he slipped inside the ring of her entrance and felt her inner walls cling to him, he damn near sagged at the sensation. Ira shook even harder against him, and he held her closer.

"I'm not feelin' this position," she panted, shifting in a way that indicated discomfort rather than impatience.

"One second," he whispered, and then he surged the rest of the way inside. Her gasp almost made him come, and the gloved, damp heat of her almost made him too weak to stand. He never wanted to leave her wet depths ever.

"Hold on to me," he murmured, grasping her securely around the waist as she wrapped her arms around his neck. He pulled her off the small table, barely registering how it wobbled once free of her weight, and then walked a few steps to rest her back against the wall beside the furniture. Walking while inside of her had sent zings of pleasure along his dick and throughout the rest of his body, especially since she'd squeezed her inner walls as hard around his cock as she had her arms around his neck.

Max kissed Ira lazily and thoroughly, sliding out of her body with all deliberate speed before taking his sweet time entering her again. He gloried in her ample ass in his hands, in her fingers sliding through his hair, in her glazed gaze locking with his. She started growing heavy, but Max didn't care. He wasn't letting her go for anything. He was strong enough to hold her.

"Faster," Ira breathed, tugging his hair. "Please, *faster*."

Not too fast, though. He increased his speed so that his thrusts were still gentle, if more frequent. Ira moaned and threw her head back against the wall, presenting the thick column of her throat. He gripped it with his teeth, groaning when she clenched around his cock in reaction, and he tugged the bodice of the gorgeous canary dress down her torso to reveal the black strapless bra she wore. He growled his momentary frustration before licking the perspiration that had pooled between her breasts. It was salty on his tongue.

"Off," he muttered, yanking the lingerie down. Her breasts plopped free, her nipples dark and hard. His mouth watered. Max bent forward to take one in his mouth, but the collar of his shirt choked his neck, bringing him to an abrupt halt.

"Guh—"

"*Off*," Ira echoed, tugging at his shirt. She squeezed her thighs around his hips tightly and he bit back a moan at the hot, soft flesh of her hold around him. He helped her remove the offending cloth until he was finally as topless as she was. He let her gaze at him, shuddered when her soft hands smoothed along his chest and shoulders.

"Ira," he whispered. He wanted to move again, to take them both to the stars.

"I'm going to miss you so much."

Max closed his eyes against the spring of tears that suddenly filled them. Shaking his head, he rested his forehead against hers and began his deliberate thrusting again.

"I ain't goin' nowhere for you to miss, baby."

Cupping his cheeks, Ira shook her head. "I don't want you to take me to the train station."

He paused, buried to the hilt inside of her. "Why not?"

"I won't get on the train if you do."

He grinned and blinked, uncaring a tear decided to fall down his face anyway. "Good."

"Max—"

"I don't want you to go."

"I gotta go, Max."

"Fuck that."

Ira huffed out a laugh, then a pleasured grunt when he thrust more forcefully inside of her. Her entire body jiggled deliciously, and he gripped her ass harder in his hands.

"Like that?" Ira asked teasingly.

"Not nearly so pleasurably," Max corrected with a grin.

She grinned also, but then her expression turned somber again. "Clean break."

"Ain't gonna be clean. Gonna be messy as hell," Max promised.

"Were you like this with Shirleen?"

"Ain't feel like this with Shirleen or anyone else," he said plainly. He thrust hard into her again.

She kissed him, letting her tongue find his. She stroked him with the rhythm that he slid in and out of her. He felt his orgasm coil at the base of his spine, in his balls. He wanted to give her everything. He wanted all of her in return.

"You gotta let me go," Ira said once she broke the kiss. She didn't move far from him, her lips brushing against his as she spoke. "I gotta go."

Max sank back inside of her and then paused, his jaw clenching. She was right and he knew it, but he was fucking *tired* of everything he held dear leaving him. Except, unlike with the others, Ira could come back.

He had to have faith she would.

Instead of answering verbally, he resumed thrusting, keeping his eyes inexorably locked on hers. She began to close hers, but he grunted and stopped thrusting.

"Look at me, Ira."

She squeezed her eyes harder. "I can't."

"If you gotta leave, you gotta look at me while you do."

"I'm not leavin' now."

"Yeah, you are. I feel you doin' it," he said, and his tone was more sad than accusatory. "Stay with me a little longer, just for right now."

"Then I can keep my eyes closed?"

He had to laugh. It was quiet, barely heard above her harsh breaths as she clung to the precipice of release. He could recognize her brink now: her face grew tight, her lips parted, her pussy clenched him in a death grip he never wanted to leave.

"You open those eyes, girl, and watch me love you."

After a moment, gorgeous brown eyes looked back at him. Ira's body became pliant, softening in his hold. Jesus Christ, but she was everything he hadn't realized he'd wanted or could even have: sweet, decadently plump, caring, funny, *single*.

His. She was his. Whether he took her to the train station tomorrow or not; whether they never spoke to each other ever again, she was *his*. His one, his love, *his* dream come true.

Overcome with emotion, Max pressed his lips to hers and began thrusting in earnest. If she were leaving tomorrow without him, he'd make sure she'd take everything of him with her.

Twenty-Three

You know, out of all my girls, you were the very last one I thought would disappoint me.

Well, it looks like you were right.

Ira winced as the conversation's climax replayed in her head, a reaction she still had with each continuous loop even two weeks after the live confrontation. Sighing, she plopped down wet clay on the pottery wheel, her right foot pressing down on the pedal to get the contraption moving. She'd already messed up before she'd even begun—she knew better than to start before she had an idea of what she wanted to make. Instead, she watched the gray glob of clay spin, her hands hovering over the wheel as she waited for inspiration to come.

Her breath shuddered out of her body, and the pottery wheel swam in her vision as tears pricked her eyes. Ever since she'd met Max, tears had been easier to come by, and Ira wasn't sure she liked that very much. Her birthday weekend had reconnected herself to her emotions in a way she hadn't anticipated. She'd gone all in, yes, but she hadn't gotten out yet, even if she hadn't seen Max in the flesh for just as long.

However, it seemed a piece of him had come back with her.

She placed an unconscious hand on her abdomen and let out a snort. Of *all* of the Jackson girls, of course she'd be one and done in the conception department. Apparently, her low-dosage birth control had been no match for Max's virility, or the condoms they'd used that weekend . . . or that one time against the wall in his condo's vestibule when they hadn't used any protection at all. It'd been Ira who'd noticed first. She'd made a flippant comment about how sticky she'd felt between her thighs and how wet she must've still been for him. He'd been the one to suck in a sharp breath and apologize for being too selfish and irresponsible to protect her properly.

"Birth control," she'd trilled, even as her heart had swooped down into her belly, and then below that to splat at her feet. She hadn't been all that vigilant about taking it that weekend, and she couldn't remember taking her dosage for that day.

"Ain't perfect," he'd replied, pressing a hand on her belly. Then he'd whispered something so softly, she'd known he hadn't intended for her to hear. But she had.

I hope it ain't.

Ira closed her eyes at that memory and got her emotions in check. Had it not been for her aunt's pot roast that fateful Sunday night, Ira didn't know when she would've recognized the signs of her condition. Probably after this missed cycle would she have started paying attention to her body. She'd had off-and-on spotting since that birthday weekend, enough where she was curious, but not to the point of alarm since she'd spotted that way before and she'd certainly not been pregnant then. She'd also had mild symptoms: some discomfort and tenderness in her breasts, some fatigue, but she'd chalked that last up to the long, nightly conversations she and Max had via video conferencing. Her alertness had gone way low, to the point she'd have to stop by The Grind to get a coffee before going into work.

She wasn't the world's biggest coffee drinker.

But that pot roast, one of her favorite meals, had sent her rushing to her aunt and uncle's half-bath and heaving into the toilet. Her aunt had insisted they call 9-1-1 while her cousin Jerome wiped her face and her uncle Elias talked his wife down from the ledge. But then Jerome had tried to tease her about not being so close since he didn't want to catch whatever bug must be floating around at that urgent care of hers, and she'd gripped her cousin's forearm so tightly in her shock that he'd cried out in pained surprise.

"Ain't no bug," she'd breathed, her eyes growing wide.

"What?" her cousin had replied, managing to ease her grip, and then he'd scoffed. "Must be! Ain't like you can be pregnant!"

"WHAT!" Aunt Dot had cried. "*Pregnant!*"

Nobody had eaten the pot roast that night, after all.

In fact, the smell of red meat now set Ira off something fierce, which actually upset her greatly because she could *really* use a greasy burger right about now. She snorted to herself. Maybe that was what she should sculpt now, an homage to a double bacon cheeseburger with honey mustard sauce.

"Nah," she said, still chuckling to herself as she scooped up water into her palm from the bucket at her side and poured it over the stiffening clay. She'd just make a bowl. Bowls were reliable and simple and gave her something mindless, yet productive, to do with her hands.

Of course, her phone decided the perfect time to ring was when she was fingers- and palms-deep in the clay. Groaning aloud, she scooted her wheeled stool over to the table where she'd set her belongings, thankful, at least, she'd had the presence of mind to keep her phone outside of her bag. She checked the name on the screen.

Gideon.

Groaning at her cousin's penchant for calling at inopportune times, Ira used her tablet's stylus to answer the phone and put the device on speaker.

"Yes, ma'am."

"Hey! Where you at?"

Ira cut her eyes at the phone and wheeled her way back to the pottery wheel. "South Carolina. Where are you?"

"South Carolina! I'm here, bih!"

Ira immediately smiled. "Really? I didn't know you were coming!" It was Labor Day weekend. Normally, Gideon had someplace far more exotic to be than her home state.

"I wanted to surprise you, but I wasn't sure you were home. Tonight's pottery studio night, right? Unless you have a hot date?"

Her snort came out strangled because a sob tried to take its place. "I'm hardly out on a date, Gids."

"Why? Max turned you out that good?"

"Bye, Gideon."

"Dang! Full name and not a hint of warmth! What I say? I thought y'all were carrying on this love story for the ages via the *internets*."

Ira's smile wobbled and she couldn't answer for a moment. She knew if she opened her mouth, a sob would escape, so she had to wait until that urge passed. However, her cousin was too perceptive, and her jocular tone turned empathetic.

"What's wrong, Ira?" she asked. "Do I gotta beat Max's ass?"

Good ol' Gideon, bringing forth a laugh instead of the tears that had threatened. She sobered quickly, however, and was settled enough that she could speak without sounding like marbles had been shoved down her throat.

"No, not his ass. Might have to beat mine, though."

"Yours? Girl, whyever for?"

Ira rolled her eyes at Gideon's affected speech but sighed. "Are you driving?"

"Yeah?"

"You might want to pull over."

Gideon sucked her teeth at that. "For what? Girl, what in the world could you possibly tell me that could make me cause a wreck? Shit, you pregnant or somethin'?"

She began to laugh, and Ira did, too, mainly because Gideon's incredulity matched her brother's over such a thing being possible.

Then suddenly, Gideon's sound cut off, and Ira frowned at the abrupt silence.

"Gids?" Still nothing. Frowning more, Ira rolled back over to the table to see the call was still connected. "Gideon?"

Gideon's voice came back on the line, but it was sharp in its bewilderment. "*Are* you pregnant?"

"What happened?" Ira asked, alarm coloring her voice.

"I'm in a damn Staples parking lot so I don't freak out over the fact *you're pregnant!*"

"A minute ago, you were laughing!"

"Yeah, well, shit ain't funny anymore!" Gideon said, huffing. "I mean, of all—"

"Don't," Ira interrupted. "I already heard that from your mom."

Gideon made an indignant sound. "Well, damn, though! I mean, when Jerome suggested I come home, I didn't—*really*?"

Ira smiled softly at that revelation. Jerome really was a sweetheart. A week ago, he'd come with her to her appointment that confirmed the pregnancy, but he hadn't said much other than to assure the doctor he was *not* the father. The mix-up's hilarity had been just what she'd needed to relieve the tension that had grown inside of her. The other thing Jerome had done was *not* ask for details about the hows and whys of the surprise conception.

"When you're ready," he'd made her promise during their post-appointment lunch at a local Applebee's. "But regardless, you know I got you."

His lack of judgment—for good or ill—had been just what she'd needed to hear. And while she still hadn't drummed up the wherewithal to tell Gideon or Murphy, the latter who'd been busy recording for various artists while rehearsing for her gig at this year's Emmys and thus was nigh unreachable, Jerome's "when you're ready" had given her permission to have breathing room for herself to process this upcoming and massive change in her life.

So long to that, now that Gideon knew!

"I was gonna get you and Murphy on a conference call and—"

"Max?"

"Max?"

"You haven't told him."

Gideon's tone was a statement, not a question, and Ira's hackles rose. "No."

"Obviously," Gideon muttered. "He's not—" She cut herself off and sighed. "It's none of my business."

"You're right about that," Ira snapped.

"I'm sorry."

Ira waved away the apology even though Gideon couldn't see her. "I'd wanted to tell him first before I told anyone else. But I didn't want to do it over the phone and . . . I . . ." She released a shuddering breath. "Please don't tell him, Gideon. He deserves to hear it from me."

"Yeah," Gideon said, her tone soft once more. "Let me get out of this parking lot before the po-po come and I become a hashtag."

"GIDEON!" Ira cried. Her cousin really could be irreverent.

"I'm just sayin'. This the South and I'm drivin' a nice car. I ain't tryna go out like that."

"Oh, Lord! Just drive safely!"

Shaking her head, Ira used the stylus to end the call then wheeled herself back to the pottery wheel. Her clay was a hardened clump now, ruined. Sighing, she threw it away and washed her hands in a nearby basin. Ira didn't bother throwing more clay. She knew where the Staples was, and it was only a few lights down from the pottery studio. Instead, she cleaned up her space, a little annoyed her two hours of quiet would now be interrupted, and wiped off her stylus and phone before sitting at the worktable and queuing up an audiobook about first-time pregnancy on her tablet. As she listened, she pulled out a notebook from her bag and began to sketch. She was no grand artist, but sketching was a great way for her to work out what she'd want to create with the clay. That this was where she should've started, as she did have sketches that hadn't been tried yet, didn't hit her with force like it probably would've if she weren't so distracted. Hell, if she hadn't been so distracted, she would've chosen one earlier this afternoon or even yesterday to work on for today. She shelled out a nice penny to book this private studio time here, but Ira felt it was well worth it.

Even today when she'd gotten little done. It was good to be alone with her non-worrisome thoughts.

Ironically, the distractedness that had been her friend for the majority of the two weeks had decided to leave her be once she'd put pencil to paper. What had started forming was, of all things, a baby bottle. It wasn't the most gorgeous of baby bottles, but Ira thought it might make for a really good "Baby's First Bank," something different from a traditional piglet. Since bottles usually provided sustenance for the body, the bottle bank could begin her child's financial nourishment.

She smiled to herself at her cleverness. Yes, this would be her next project, and maybe she'd make it larger than the sketch so it could last her baby at least into toddlerhood.

Ira's phone vibrating broke her concentration briefly, but she shot off a quick reply text to Gideon, letting her know which room in the arts building she was using. She hadn't sunk back to the deep level of focus she'd been in earlier, so she was able to hear the knock on the door. She didn't look up, though, simply calling for Gideon to enter. As soon as she was finished drawing this line, she'd greet her cousin properly.

Except, as soon as the door closed after opening, Ira knew it wasn't Gideon in the room.

Maybe her pregnancy made her more sensitive to the air and how it shifted. Her senses were definitely heightened, and this was not how Gideon Jackson felt when she entered a room. The tension that coiled in her body now was too tight; her heart beat too furiously. Her skin prickled, primed to be touched. And, good Lord, even her mouth watered in anticipation of slaked desire.

Her throat constricted around the heart that had leapt into it and she could barely breathe as footsteps grew closer to her. She couldn't look up from her notepad, though, too afraid to meet her guest in the eye. Her body flamed when they made it to her side, and she trembled as the person sank down to be eye level with her.

"Ira."

Max's voice sounded so different live, tangible. Resonant. They'd been playing phone tag for the past few days, which had worked in her favor because she hadn't been all that ready to talk to him. In her defense, he'd been the elusive one first; on the other hand, if she hadn't encouraged him to look up his grandmother and brother, he wouldn't have been so single-minded and unavailable because of his search. However, Ira couldn't begrudge him for it. He'd needed to discover the only family he had left.

Or the family he *thought* he had left.

Her hand went to her middle before she could catch herself and she could feel his unblinking gaze upon the back of that hand.

"I heard you," he said in a soft voice. "On the phone. I heard you say you were pregnant."

She nodded because her throat was still too tight to speak.

"It's mine."

She nodded again, this time looking down at the floor between their feet. His loafers were brown leather underneath gray slacks that still had a crease line in them. His knees were so close to her hip they'd brush against each other if she shifted a little more to her right. She didn't move, though. The cocktail of emotions she felt could do naught but root her to the spot.

"And you were gonna tell me at some point? Before the baby was out and about and walking?"

Now she cut her eyes to him. "Max!"

"I'm just—" He sighed roughly and bent his head. "Sorry. That was rude. But in the three months since we've been apart, and all the conversations we've had, never once—"

"I didn't even find out until a week ago."

Max sighed and nodded. "Okay." He placed a hand over his mouth and sighed again, looking off into the middle distance over her shoulder. "Okay."

She turned to face him fully. The haunted look in his eyes seemed to have more to do with whatever he'd been discovering than her revelation. Taking a chance, she cupped his face in her hands. He closed his eyes and sank into her touch, leaning his cheek into one palm.

"I'm not my father."

"Damn right you're not," Ira agreed, frowning. How could he ever think that?

"You wouldn't run off with my child and never tell me. You'd never raise him without me."

"No, we'd work something out and—"

"What's there to work out? You're carryin' my baby. Seems pretty worked out to me."

She frowned deeper. "But we're not in a relationship."

"The hell we ain't," Max said, his tone indignant as he pulled his face from her hands. "Between these last three months and that baby inside you, I think we're as tied up as we could possibly be, don't you?" He raised an eyebrow at her. "Do you need me to put a ring on it to make it official?"

Ira scoffed and rolled her eyes at him. "Come on! Be serious, Max."

Just when she'd thought the last thing she'd expected to see was Max Worthington in her pottery studio, he pulled out a velvet box and revealed a glittering ring inside.

Twenty-Four

Nothing about this reunion was going to plan.

Nevertheless, Max was more assured than ever that this was the path he was supposed to travel, and Ira Jackson was supposed to be by his side while he did. The boondoggled expression on her face made him smile. No doubt that was what he'd looked like twenty minutes ago when he'd heard her confess her pregnancy over Gideon's speakerphone. It was a good thing they'd been at a light when that bomb had dropped, or Gideon probably would've run into something or someone. He'd been able to convince her to pull into a parking lot per her cousin's suggestion, especially since this was a rental under his name and, while he had the money to pay for a replacement, there were now much better uses for it instead.

Like a college fund.

He huffed out a wild laugh at the twists and turns his life had taken since Ira had entered it. Most had been great. Some had been difficult to maneuver, like beginning to truly process his mother's assault and murder at his father's hands. Some had been full of grief, such as discovering his grandmother Violet Capshaw had passed away over ten years ago and he'd known nothing about it. Some had been full of relief, like the fact his good ol' father had been in a bar fight a few years after killing his mother and had lost—permanently. Yet, perhaps the most rewarding turn was actually finding his brother—his *Navy SEAL* brother—who was just as eager to meet as Max was.

He wanted Ira to be there with him when he did. Initially, he hadn't planned on even bringing up marriage until after, whether she'd decided to go with him or not. But now, Max really hoped she'd agree to go with him as his future wife, especially since she was already the future mother of his child.

He laughed again, which apparently startled Ira out of her stupor because her eyes finally met his again.

"Max?"

He let his laughs fade away and he shook his head. "Nothing's funny and everything is."

Ira shrugged helplessly and closed the lid on the ring box. "This isn't funny."

"It's not," he agreed. "This is the most serious thing I've ever done in my life."

Ira looked at the ring box that was still held out to her. She frowned at it more. "You were planning to ask me anyway."

"Yes."

"You just walk around with that in your pocket?"

He chuckled. "No. I had it out because I'd showed it to Gideon. You know how Gideon is."

She smiled a little. "Yes. So, you talked about marriage to me with Gideon?"

He nodded. "I asked her what kind of jewelry you'd like. I had to bribe her with so many things to keep her from spilling the beans to you."

"Her choice of whatever Dream Dude she wanted?"

"She already had that," Max said with a snort. "She gets to name our first child."

Ira scowled severely at him. "I get to override that."

It wasn't a question, and Max nodded with a laugh, consenting to her terms. "Would you settle for godmother instead?"

"She'd have to share that with Murphy," Ira said, this time her expression less displeased.

Max nodded again and put the ring in his pocket. At Ira's alarmed confusion, he grinned and stood, holding out his hand so he could help her to her feet. After a brief pause, Ira allowed his help, and he immediately drew her to his chest. Goodness, but he'd missed holding her, missed her softness and her pineapple scent. He couldn't get that through a computer screen or a phone call, and his memories weren't warm enough comforts.

"Hi," Ira murmured into his neck. "I've missed you."

"Baby, it's good to be home."

Ira squeezed him tighter. He felt hot moisture at the base of his neck and his own eyes pricked. For several long moments, they cried silently in each other's arms. It felt more cathartic for him than anything else. He stroked her back, relearning the curves of her body. The lime-green and pink scrubs she wore defined her well, making him yearn for her.

"So when Gids said she wanted to surprise me, she was really talking about you, wasn't she?"

Max chuckled and turned his face into her temple, pressing a kiss there. "All of this was her idea."

"Of course it was," Ira said, sounding tickled. "I have the best cousins ever."

"Yeah?"

Ira nodded and stepped back from him. "You heard it was Jerome's idea to have her come see me."

His expression turned sympathetic. "I gather from what you said, your aunt's not happy about this baby."

"Unmarried and pregnant by a strange man I'd only known for a weekend, no less."

"Does she know I'm white?"

Ira snorted and laughed. "She would've had a heart attack if I'd added that."

"She got something against white people?"

"I defy you to find a Black person of a certain age who wouldn't, Max."

He raised an eyebrow at her. "You mean, older than the age of one?"

She gaped at him for a minute, then she threw her head back and laughed. Max couldn't help himself, and he bent down to kiss her. She immediately melted into the kiss and his body revved up, wanting her on the nearest flat surface so they could greet each other much more properly.

Nevertheless, she pulled back, still laughing lightly, and Max smiled at her.

"I can't believe you said that!"

"Mama Worthington's a Black woman 'of a certain age.' She was not shy about educating me about what it'd meant to be Black back in the day, nor how rare it was that a Black woman was fostering a white child, especially for as long as she'd done. Especially in Montgomery, Alabama."

Her fingers found one of their favorite places on his body: the nape of his neck. Max closed his eyes as Ira ran her fingers through his hair there. He'd gotten a cut, which he wished he hadn't done now. He'd like the way she'd tugged on his curls when they'd been together before. He'd let his hair grow out again so she could continue that very soon.

"And now, you're about to have a Black child," Ira whispered. "At least, not a white one."

"Yeah. That, apparently, runs in the family too."

She peered at him. "I don't understand."

"Means I'm an uncle to a niece and a nephew. They have a Black mother."

Her eyes widened, then she let out a whoop and hugged him so tightly the air burst from his lungs. Chuckling, Max hugged her back, tears coming to his eyes as the full ramifications of everything hit him. He realized Ira hadn't been the only one discovering family a week ago, for that had been when he'd gotten the courage to call the number a private investigator had given him over a month ago. He'd kept Ira up to speed about his search, but he'd not told her he'd made the call. She'd been so supportive throughout all of this, staying on the phone with him all night as he'd cried over what Mama Worthington had told him about what she'd known of his family. They'd originally been from Huntsville. His mother, Hilary Keller, had been a server at several diners and truck stops. His father, Clyde Capshaw, had been a truck driver; and his grandmother Violet had been a receptionist at a general family practice. Tim had been born four years before Max and had lived in a chaotic household until Hilary had dropped Tim on Violet's doorstep and fled.

"How did she know all of this?" Ira had asked.

"My grandmother and Mama Worthington had spoken," Max had said, trying to keep his tone light despite the ache in his heart. "And they'd decided, for my safety, to keep me with Mama Worthington since they couldn't find my dad and they didn't want to put Tim in danger."

"But your dad died some years later," Ira had reminded him. "Why didn't you go live with them then?"

Max had shrugged even though he'd known the answer then and it hadn't changed in the over twenty years since. "Mama Worthington was my family by then. And, well, I'd believed my father when he'd said they'd hate Mama; and if they'd hate Mama, they'd definitely hate me because I'm the reason she fled. And then they'd blame me for not saving Mama . . . at least, my brother would. No matter how Mama Worthington had tried to assure me they wouldn't, I couldn't take that chance."

"And nobody called to tell you she'd died?"

"No. By this point, I was out the system. The state didn't keep tabs like that anymore, and I don't think anyone else had known about the arrangement between my grandmother and foster mother. It just slipped through the cracks."

Truthfully, he'd just typed in his grandmother's name into a search engine and her obituary had popped up immediately, along with articles in the local newspaper about her and his brother. That was how he'd learned his brother had entered the Navy; and from there, he'd turned the search over to the PI. When the PI had returned with contact information, Max had sat on it for weeks before finally doing something about it.

He'd never been so terrified as when he'd listened to the phone ring before someone picked up. It'd been a feminine voice on the other end when it'd had, and Max had been so torn between hoping someone would answer and someone wouldn't that he'd been struck silent when he'd heard the pleasant greeting.

"Hello?" the woman had asked again, not impatient, exactly, but not in the mood for any games either.

He'd taken a deep breath before replying, "My name is Max Worthington. Is a Timothy Capshaw there?"

Little had Max suspected that the woman's whispered, "Oh holy hell," wouldn't be a harbinger of doom, but rather great joy.

"Tim doesn't hate me," Max whispered, coming out of his memories, his throat thick. "He doesn't hate me, Ira."

"Did he know about you?"

"Yes," Max said. "And, like me, it'd taken him years to start asking questions, looking for answers. Turns out, his grandmother had left him a small chest of things that he hadn't opened since her death, and it's only been recently that he's had the courage to go through it."

"Your grandmother too."

Max nodded. "Yeah. That's true. I'm sad I never got a chance to meet her. She sounded like a great lady. Too bad her son wasn't shit."

"Well, if all he was put on this earth to do was help to create you, then he wasn't complete shit, was he?"

He smiled and pressed another long kiss to her temple. "I really, *really*, need you to be my wife."

"That badly, huh?"

"Desperately."

She kissed his neck, then pulled back to meet his gaze. He framed her face in his hands and gave her an unwavering look.

"You don't need to give me an answer now. There's a lot of things happening, a lot of changes on the horizon, but I'd really like to marry you. And if you want to wait until after the baby's born, that's fine too—"

"I think I do," Ira interrupted. "Want to marry you, that is."

"Okay," he said, his heart feeling like fireworks had gone off inside of it.

"But can we still slow down?" Ira asked, then chuckled dryly. "As slow as we can, considering we're going to be parents in about six-seven months' time?"

"Parenthood, then matrimony."

"Maybe not that perfectly sequential, but yes."

"There has to be an order, Ira."

"If you hear my aunt tell it, we fucked that up but good."

Max rolled his eyes. "I heard your aunt on the phone that day, Ira. She's more upset by the impulsiveness, by my guess. She thinks you aren't serious about what you did, you don't understand the consequences you now face. She wanted you to find a good man, not a stranger she thinks you'll never see again."

"Oh, look at you, being all cocky."

He grinned, letting her jest roll off him. "Nobody said your search had to be long, or that there needed to be an extended probationary period for you to believe you'd found one. Gideon said your instincts were good. We've been in melody and harmony since that first conversation."

She nodded as if conceding the point.

"So let's make some sweet music together for the rest of our lives."

She groaned and chortled. "That was so damn corny!"

"You love me anyway."

"You got me there."

"I'd like to 'get' you somewhere else. Preferably onto a soft, flat surface with no clothes on."

"Oh, my Lord."

Twenty-Five

The neighborhood park was empty when they arrived, and part of Ira was glad for it. Putting the car in park and killing the engine, she looked over to Max sitting in the front passenger's seat of her car. His expression was tight, his eyes a little bloodshot behind his rectangular glasses, and his knuckles were white thanks to the death grip he had on the "oh-shit" handle above him.

"Baby, breathe."

Ira took his free hand, which he clutched with the same verve as the handle. She hissed in a breath, and he eased his hold, but only by a fraction. He closed his eyes and released a long exhalation.

"I can't do this."

"Boy, we did *not* wake up and leave my nice, *comfortable* bed at *seven* in the morning in order to leave by *eight* in the morning so we could meet your brother at *nine* in the morning, for you *not* to meet him after all. I did *not* drive an hour to *Orangeburg, South Carolina*, on a Sunday for nothing. You're meeting your family, Max."

"I already have my family. They're in this car with me right now."

Heart melting, Ira lifted his hand to her lips and kissed his knuckles. Some color returned to his hand, and she placed it on her chest.

"But there's more family on the way, baby, and that's not a bad thing. Don't be afraid at the chance of love. If I'd been, I would've never gotten on that train and met you all those months ago."

He seemed to relax some at that. "What I would've missed out on."

"Yeah," Ira agreed, smiling softly. "You've spoken to your brother several times now. He seems like good people, right?"

"Right."

"And his wife? Your sister-in-law?"

"She's really nice. Funny too."

"And your niece and nephew?"

Max's smile grew so large that hers answered in brightness. "Smart as all get out, especially baby girl Violet. She said she couldn't wait to meet 'Unca Max.'"

Leaning forward, Ira kissed his cheek underneath his glasses. "Then let's go, *Unca Max*. Let's meet the rest of your family."

"Our family," he said quietly.

Her heart was a veritable puddle now. "Our family."

They headed to the swings and they each sat down in one. She looked at the empty merry-go-round, the still slide, the silent monkey bars. In three or four years, she and Max might be at a similar playground watching their child discover each of these wonders. She breathed deeply at the prospect.

"This is apparently where my brother and sister-in-law come all the time when they visit her parents," Max said after a moment. "Just them and their kids for a bit of private family time before everybody descends on her parents' house. Apparently, it's not far."

"It's a really nice neighborhood."

"It is," Max agreed. "Reminds me of Mama Worthington's."

"Yours."

He chuckled slightly. "I could never really let myself think of it that way. Knowing I was a foster kid."

"But they let you stay for all of those years without a formal adoption?"

"Apparently. I don't know the particulars and I never asked. I knew I was more than a check to her, though. It was probably at Grandma Violet's insistence I didn't leave her, now that I think about it."

Ira stood and walked behind him, wrapping her arms around his shoulders. He leaned his head against hers and sighed.

"I need this to go well, Ira. I . . . just need this to go well."

"Have faith."

"I have you," he replied. "Same thing."

Ira smiled and squeezed his shoulders. "Just think: if Gids and my aunt could pull it together for a few hours, there's all the hope in the world for you and your brother."

Max's shoulders relaxed slightly upon hearing that point. "That's definitely a perspective I can use."

She and Max had had dinner with all her family save Murphy yesterday evening, and it'd gone rather well. They'd met at a neutral location in Charleston, Ira's favorite restaurant Poogan's Porch. Max had managed to reserve a private room for them, and it was the first time Gideon and Aunt Dot had been in the same room for years. Initially, the tension had been so thick Ira could barely breathe. But then, Max, in full view of her family, had calmed her down and assured her he would be there no matter what happened after this dinner. Evidently, that'd been what Elias and Dorothy Jackson had needed to hear, for their demeanor had warmed considerably after that. Even when he'd revealed he owned a male escort service, her parents had managed to remain polite.

"And are you one of these, uh, 'Dream Dudes?'" Aunt Dot had asked with some edge.

"No," Max had replied. "But even if I were, who I am and how I feel for your niece is very real."

"Good answer," Jerome had said. "How long that remains true, though, remains to be seen."

"As with any relationship," Max had said in return. "I can't promise together forever, but I can promise I'll give my best effort to keep your cousin happy."

"Naw, happy ain't good enough," Uncle Elias had countered, shaking his head. "I need her ecstatic."

"Blissful," Jerome had returned.

"Euphoric," Elias had volleyed back.

"Ebullient."

"*Oooh*, I like that one, 'Rome," Gideon had said, her first words since the long hugs she'd given her father and brother. "How about jubilant?"

"Yes," Uncle Elias had commended. "Nothin' less than all the above for any of my kids."

And once that commandment had settled upon the table, Aunt Dot had plucked a complimentary biscuit from the basket in the middle of the table and began to butter it. "Well, very nice to see my insistence on a 'Word-of-the-Day' has finally borne fruit."

It'd been Gideon's snort that had set the rest of the room off into raucous laughter, and they'd managed an enjoyable meal for the next two hours. Even at the end of it, Gideon and Aunt Dot had managed a quick buss to each other's cheeks. Ira had no illusions that they'd start talking regularly again, but at least there might be a return of holiday calls between them—New Year's at the very least.

The crunch of gravel from the park's parking lot broke Ira from her thoughts, but she didn't turn. Neither did Max.

"Hello? Max?"

It was a feminine voice; but given the way Max stiffened in her hold, it was one he recognized. He suddenly began trembling. Ira cooed in his ear before calling out, "Yes. It's Max. I'm Ira, his partner. Can you give us a moment?"

"That's fine," the woman said, her voice a little thick. "I'm Bevin, Tim's wife. We just wanted to make sure and not assume it was y'all."

"'We,'" Max croaked.

"Yeah, baby," Ira said, placing her smiling cheek against Max's slack one. "Tim's here. And if his wife is speaking for him, I can only assume he's just as nervous as you are right now. Does that make you feel a little better?"

"Not really."

Nevertheless, Max stood. Ira let her arms drop but kept her hands on his back, bracing him. His shoulders rose and fell with the deep breath he took, and then he turned to face her.

"Stay with me," he said.

"Always."

He kissed her forehead softly, lingeringly. She threaded her right hand into his left, then stood next to him and gazed ahead.

The Capshaws were a striking couple: she plump and the color of midnight and he a poster boy for an All-American with his big, muscular body and blond hair. But he stared at Max as if he'd seen a ghost, and one look at Max showed the same for him.

"Good lord," Tim said in a deep voice that sounded so much like Max's that she looked at Max to confirm he hadn't actually been the one to speak. "He really did spit you out."

Max blinked, his eyes widening. "Really?"

"Yeah, man, you really look just like Clyde."

Max grimaced and Ira squeezed his hand. "Sorry."

"Naw, would be like Clyde to give Ma one massive 'fuck you' for leaving him like she did."

"She didn't live long enough for her to see me grow into his face," Max said bitterly.

"That ain't your fault either," Tim said, and his voice wobbled a bit. "I'm sorry; I'm fuckin' this all the way up."

"You really are free with these f-bombs, dear."

"Sorry, sugar," Tim said, looking down at his wife with contrition stark in his eyes, then turned back to Max. "Let's start all of this over."

The blond man stepped forward, his wife's hand still in his, and he raised the free one. "Max? I'm Tim. Nice to meet you."

Max didn't step forward, nor did he take Tim's hand. Instead, he looked into Tim's face as if mesmerized.

"And *you're* like a male version of Mama," Max said after a moment. "Fair and pale. Same green eyes too."

"Keller eyes," Tim said, dropping his hand, but he grinned. "Grandma called them that."

Max closed his eyes and Ira felt him falter. She braced him as best she could, but Tim breached the space between them and grabbed Max's shoulders.

"I wish," Max began, then he shook his head. "I'm sorry," he ultimately said, his voice so thick with tears that Ira's heart broke. "I'm sorry I took Mama from you. I'm sorry I couldn't save her."

"Aw, hell," Tim muttered, right before pulling him into a hard hug. The sounds of twin deep, soul-wracking shudders had tears coming to Ira's eyes, and she backed away to give them privacy. She grieved with them and felt annoyed at her helplessness that she couldn't fix it for either of them, but particularly for Max.

A gentle hand on her shoulder made Ira look up to see the other woman. Her striking, golden eyes against her sable skin took Ira's breath away.

"Hey, I'm Bevin, Tim's wife."

"Ira," she replied. "It's nice to meet you."

Bevin nodded and sighed, looking at the two men who were still crying and embracing. "I really could use a hug myself."

"Oh, not just me, then?"

They laughed, and then they hugged fiercely. Ira suspected this was because they wanted to comfort their men, but also share a moment of solidarity with each other. Though Bevin was more intimate with her husband processing this newfound family, Ira had been shouldering the bulk of everything remotely, unable to comfort Max physically. This hug was a cathartic release for her, and it was with someone who also understood.

"Thank you for being there for him," Bevin said after a few moments. "Max. From the stories Tim has told me about his parents, I don't blame their mother for fleeing. But sometimes the devil wins despite everyone's best efforts."

"They lost out on a mother and each other because of that man," Ira replied, pulling out of the hug but staying close to Bevin.

"Yes, but the universe decided if the only good Clyde Capshaw did in his sorry-ass life was help create two upstanding men, that would be enough to balance everything out."

Ira had to laugh. "I told Max the same thing."

They walked over to the swings and sat down. Looking behind her, Ira noticed the men head to her car. She took her key out of her purse and unlocked the door using the fob. They waved their hands in thanks to her.

"You and Max have spoken about this a lot?"

"As much as we could," Ira said, "but not like you and Tim must've."

Bevin snorted. "Please. I've hardly seen my husband all week! Between our work and those two talkin' every night for hours. We learned quickly that video chats would be invaded by the kids, so they stick to the phone. He sits out every night on that balcony and they just . . . talk. I know about family, but then just regular things. They share the same parents but they're little better than strangers. That doesn't sit right with my husband, Ira. He *hates* it. For years, he thought he was the only family he had. Then he'd found his SEAL family and that helped, and then mine came along. But this? I've prayed every night since Max called that they actually *liked* each other as people, not just because they share DNA."

"Well, it's a good thing Tim has you," Ira said. "This kind of revelation rocks foundations."

"Yes," Bevin agreed. "But he's also mad at himself for not discovering this years ago when he'd had the means to do so the entire time."

Ira shook her head. "Everything happens when it's supposed to happen, if it's supposed to happen."

"Chile, amen to that."

As their men got to know each other, Ira and Bevin did too. Ira caught Bevin up on what had been happening in the Lowcountry while Bevin discussed being an entrepreneur and continuing her aim to turn The Grind, a coffeehouse she and a group of friends had started right in Charleston, into a regional chain while being a mother to two precocious children under the age of eight. She graciously let Ira have a fangirl moment and gush about that, Ira telling the other woman that had been hers and her coworkers' breakfast spot since forever.

Bevin also gave a brief sketch of her courtship with Tim Capshaw, or Timothy as she'd call him sometimes whenever the vignette was particularly full of, in Bevin's words, "ain't-shit" shenanigans.

"So, yours was a quick courtship too?" Ira asked after some time.

Bevin snickered. "That man had me at hello, and I did my level best to deny it. But he was persistent and wouldn't let me hide from the truth." She then sighed and shook her head, stretching her short legs out in front of her. "These Capshaw men, Ira. From my experience with Tim and what you've told me about Max, they love something fierce. Quiet as it's kept, they probably got their daddy's passion, but they just channel it the right way."

"And are man enough to accept it."

Bevin huffed and nodded. "Amen to that too."

They sat in silence, rocking on the swings. There were the occasional cars that came by the park and crossed through the intersection. A few honked horns, compelling Bevin to smile and wave. Ira closed her eyes, enjoying the peace of the morning.

"My mama wanted me to invite you and Max to the house if you wanted to stay for a late lunch/early dinner," Bevin said. "We decided to skip church today, especially since we saw Pastor Kerry yesterday, and, well, we wanted to spend some uninterrupted time with y'all."

"Your parents will be there?"

"They did go to church. They'll be back after that. They're real excited to meet Max." She chuckled. "Mama even made him a red velvet cake."

Ira laughed. "Really?"

Bevin laughed as well, clearly very tickled by the backstory. "She threatened my father with no batter for the next ten cakes she baked if a piece of either Tim's hummingbird or Max's red velvet came up missing, and my daddy's *dead serious* about his cake batter!"

"And with the holidays coming up, that woulda been a major loss."

The women looked behind them to see the brothers approaching. Goodness, but they even had the same gait. They were power personified. And while they looked so completely unalike in features, their vibes indicated their relation.

The women stood and met the men halfway; but when Tim swooped down to gather Ira in a large hug, she squeaked her surprise, her eyes growing wide.

"Welcome to the family!"

Ira laughed and hugged him in return. "Uh, thanks?"

Tim's deep laughter warmed her from the inside. It felt so familiar, like Max's, that she relaxed against him. Tim loosened his grip on her, but the hug remained sweet and welcoming.

"Thank you for lovin' my brother, ma'am."

Ira blamed her hormones for how easily she came to tears nowadays. "Oh hell."

He chuckled, squeezed her briefly, then stepped back. Ira looked over to see Max and Bevin sharing their own intimate hug, and Ira had to look away. In one fell swoop, Max had gained a brother, a sister, a niece, and a nephew, and, apparently, another set of parents if Bevin's mother had gone through all the trouble to make his favorite cake sight unseen.

"And the little one inside you," Tim continued. "It's gonna get so much love you all will be swimmin' in it."

Bevin's gasp was loud and excited. "You're *pregnant!*" She didn't wait for an answer, hugging Max so hard she rocked him, then she punched his biceps.

"Ow!"

"You two impatient 'Bama boys—y'all are definitely brothers!"

"Why wait? That's my motto," Tim said with not a trace of remorse.

"You would," Bevin grumbled. "Don't give a body time to acclimate or *nothin'*."

"Wife," Tim warned, wrapping an arm around Ira's shoulder. "Don't go scarin' your future sister-in-law."

The quickness with which Bevin switched from grouse to glee almost made Ira burst out laughing. "Really!"

"I haven't officially said yes, nor has there been an actual question," Ira clarified, looking at Max pointedly. He reddened while Tim waved the words away.

"Semantics and technicalities," Tim dismissed. "By this time next year, you'll be a proper Capshaw-Worthington."

Max snorted. "My name on my birth certificate is Clarke."

"*Clarke*?" Ira and Tim asked simultaneously.

"Yeah," Max said with a wry chuckle. "I was born Maximus Clarke. No middle name. Seemed Mama *really* wanted nothing to do with Clyde."

"Except, Clarke was her ma's maiden name, so, maybe she was trying to keep everything on her side of the family with you. My name, Timothy Dean, are Capshaw side names," Tim explained.

"Really?" Ira was surprised he'd have that much detail about a woman with whom he'd had even less time than Max.

Tim nodded, then proceeded to answer her unspoken question. "Grandma knew everything about everybody in our part of town. She was the genealogical expert, considering she'd worked in the one family practice for forever. And, well, Grandma made sure she told me about Ma, even if most of my personal memories of her were nothin' like Grandma's stories. Turns out, she wasn't always a drunk."

"She never drank around me," Max confirmed.

"Yeah, well," Tim muttered, and Ira felt compelled to squeeze his waist. He returned the squeeze around her shoulders, then nodded his head toward their car.

"Come on. I'm sure y'all are hungry. Mama Bevie left us some pancake batter so we can have some breakfast."

"I offered to drive them back with us—"

"Of course," Ira agreed before Max even finished his statement.

They weren't even two minutes away, and soon Ira was pulling up behind a large SUV with NAVY and "The Grind" bumper stickers in the driveway of a single-story brick house. Bevin and Tim, both seated in the back, immediately unbuckled their seatbelts, but Max was frozen once again. Ira saw Bevin squeeze his shoulder and Tim did the same to her.

"Y'all take all the time you need," Bevin said. "Front door'll be unlocked for you."

The words were enough to get Max out of the car, but he didn't follow his brother and sister-in-law into the house. Instead, he watched the structure while cuddling Ira as they leaned against her locked driver's side door.

"I was scared they weren't actually as great as they were," Max said after long, silent minutes had passed. "Afraid we'd fall apart once we met in person, that there was magic in the distance between us, talkin' on the phone. But he wants me, Ira. He loves me. His wife too. His wife's *family*. His kids. I'm wanted, Ira. Clyde was wrong. My brother loves me. Already."

"I don't know why you sound so surprised by that," Ira said, sliding her fingers into his hair behind his ears. "It only took me a day to fall in love with you."

"Well, I'll be," Max said, bending forward to kiss her gently. "Got me all happy, blissful, euphoric, *and* ebullient."

Ira giggled against his mouth. "Don't forget jubilant."

"How could I ever?"

They shared another sweet kiss, this one longer. Max then broke it with a small sigh, his forehead against hers.

"I'm ready to go in."

"You sure?"

He nodded without lifting his head from hers. "With you by my side, I'm ready for anything."

With a final nuzzle to his cheek, Ira stepped back, pulling him with her. She threaded her arm through his and took a deep breath. He did the same.

Then, as one, they headed to the front door.

Related Books

Trolling Nights

Navy SEAL Timothy Capshaw is only in Charleston, South Carolina, for the summer. He's not looking for a romance or even a hookup, but when he sees Bevin on

his first night out on the town, he knows she's the one
for him.

Coffeehouse owner Bevin Moore is the friend who
ensures everyone makes safe decisions when they go out
on their Trolling Nights, the nights where her friends
look for a weekend fling. Then she meets Tim, and she's
certain he's the most dangerous choice of all—especially
for her heart.

How will Tim convince Bevin he's the man she hasn't
known she's been looking for and that the need for her
Trolling Nights is over?

I'll Be Your Somebody

Coffeehouse entrepreneur Rosita Velez has kept her distance from Ulrich Brown from the moment she saw him on that fateful Trolling Night. Not because she thinks he's a jerk not worthy of her time—the exact opposite, in fact. He's hot, funny, honorable, intelligent—and has she mentioned hot? He's the kind of guy who looks for forever while she's focused on the here and now. Completely incompatible. Then a doomed relationship between him and another member of the Femme Crew has her offering a shoulder, then more, to the grieving Navy SEAL.

A casual arrangement is perfect for Rosita, just scratch an itch with a gorgeous guy and be about her business. But when those scratches become caresses, the one part of herself she thought she could guard forever begins to slip right out of her chest into Ulrich's waiting hands.

TROLLING NIGHTS
Excerpt

Tim pulled into her apartment complex and parked in front of her unit. He shut the car off, but he didn't move to leave. Bevin unbuckled her seatbelt, yet remained where she was as well.

"You're a damn desirable woman, Bevin Moore," Tim began, looking through the windshield at the drops that were hitting it in rapid succession. "And I think you're starting to accept that."

Her brows furrowed, displaying her confusion. "I wasn't doing anything special."

"Sweetheart, you don't have to *do* anything special to *be* special. You walk in a room and you light it up."

She smiled, touched by his words.

"That, right there," Tim said, turning so he faced her. He grasped her chin in his big hand and let his thumb touch her bottom lip. "Who wouldn't want to be around you? You're smart, Bevin. Witty. Beautiful . . ." He stopped talking and brushed the backs of his fingers against her cheek. Anything she could've possibly said evaporated on her tongue. He was beguiling her so sweetly, she could barely breathe.

"I wanted to hurt someone today."

For the second time, her mouth dropped open, and her eyes widened. "Why?"

"I didn't like the way they were looking at you," he said unapologetically. "I know it was your birthday, even if you would've let the day pass without even telling me." He eyed her comically, then he grew grave again. "But I didn't like the way you smiled at them . . . the way you pressed against them while you danced."

"They're your friends, Tim."

"And you're my woman, and I have a serious problem with sharing."

She started rolling her eyes, but Tim squeezed her chin, shaking his head. "I'm not kidding, Bevin. I'd never felt such possessiveness overtake me. I didn't want to keep you from having a good time, because if I'd touched you, I would've kept you all to myself."

His confession confused her. "I don't understand."

"I said I don't like sharing, Bevin. Tonight, I was really close to behaving like an asshole because everyone was standing in your shine and I want it only to be mine."

"But you did anyway," she said, easing her chin out his grasp and leaving the car. She heard another car door slam behind her, and seconds later, a strong, warm hand closed around her upper arm, pulling her body against a much larger and firmer one.

The rain had already plastered his hair to his head, and the fat drops sluiced the harsh planes of his skin. His sea-green eyes seemed to blaze in the wet darkness, searing her; but despite her trepidation, it wasn't of him physically hurting her. Deep inside, Bevin knew he'd never do that.

"You're mine," he said, almost drowned out by the rain, but her heart heard him loud and clear. "You belong to me. I know that's not an evolved thing to say, but that's my truth. But I also never want to make you feel trapped or stifled, so if that means keeping my distance when my possessiveness gets too overwhelming, then that's what I'll do."

Bevin couldn't feel the rain ruining her hair or soaking her woefully inadequate attire. She could only feel her nipples harden under the cool, wet weather and his eyes on her. She licked her lips and pressed further into him.

"When did you come to that decision?" she asked, lifting her hands to caress his chest. "That I belong to you?"

He closed his eyes and clenched his jaw, then turned those blazing eyes back on her. "When I saw you at The Barrel almost two months ago."

She couldn't help her feminine grin. "All the way back then?"

"Yeah, sugar," he whispered. He tucked saturated strands of her hair behind her ear. "All the way back then."

"Do I get a say in the matter?" she asked just as softly.

He grinned at her and touched his nose to hers. "You already did."

She chuckled despite herself. "Really? Where was I?"

His arms banded around her, and he brought her even closer to him. "You were leaning against the railing on the Battery giving me your very first kiss."

For more on *Trolling Nights*, visit
https://www.sjfbooks.com/crafting/tn.

Acknowledgments

Thank you to all the members on my Patreon who received the first iteration of this story back in 2016, as well as LaVerne Thompson, who was my primary beta reader then too. I truly appreciate your support and feedback. Also, many thanks to my agent, Saritza Hernandez, who's heard one version of this story or another for the past six years and has always provided invaluable guidance for me.

Many beautiful thanks to my family, particularly my sister Karma, for their continued encouragement and support of my writing.

Finally, thank you to you, dear reader, for investing your time in reading this story. I truly hope you enjoyed it.

About the Author

Savannah J. Frierson is a *USA TODAY* best-selling and award-winning author penning diverse romance and mainstream fiction full of genuine characters, authentic stories, and passionate feeling.

Find Savannah online at
https://www.sjfbooks.com/online.